...urches and weddings? Not for Mark. Not anymore.

He'd become adept at drifting from relationship to relationship, never allowing things to become too serious.

Why was he here?

A question that had nothing to do with witnessing his best friend's wedding and everything to do with moving back to his hometown.

He glanced over at Sammi, this time finding her brown eyes staring at him, brows drawn together in worry.

Her customary braid was gone today, her long dark hair left free to spill over her bare shoulders and halfway down her back, thick and glossy. He knew firsthand how decadent those silky strands felt as they flowed across his hands…his body.

He shifted in his spot to keep from remembering too deeply, knowing this was not the time or place. Later, when he slugged back his first shot of whiskey and tried to push away the horrors of the last eight years, he could afford to nurse his regrets.

Soft clapping around him made him realize the bride and groom were now in each other's arms, their lips locked together.

How soon could he get out of here?

Love conquers all.

W

Dear Reader

I was raised in a military family, surrounded by men whose love and bravery often led them into dangerous and difficult situations. My grandfather served in the Army, while my father was a career Navy man. Squadron numbers, ranks and the names of aircraft carriers might sound like Greek to most of the world, but to me they were a part of everyday life.

Both my dad and my grandfather relayed stories of triumph and heartache from their years in the service. But I suspect other tales remained buried, known only to them and those who served with them. My book's hero arose from this idea. What happens when someone tries to lock away a terrible memory, only to have it resurface in unexpected ways? What must that be like for those who love him and want to help?

Thank you for joining Mark and Sammi as they reunite after years apart. As they struggle to overcome the things which drove them apart in the first place. Best of all, this special couple rekindles a love they thought was long dead. I hope you enjoy reading about their journey as much as I enjoyed writing about it!

Sincerely

Tina Beckett

THE MAN WHO WOULDN'T MARRY

BY
TINA BECKETT

MILLS & BOON

First published in Great Britain 2012
by Mills & Boon, an imprint of Harlequin (UK) Limited.
Harlequin (UK) Limited, Eton House,
18-24 Paradise Road, Richmond, Surrey TW9 1SR

© Tina Beckett 2012

ISBN: 978 0 263 89203 1

Printed and bound in Spain
by Blackprint CPI, Barcelona

Born to a family that was always on the move, **Tina Beckett** learned to pack a suitcase almost before she knew how to tie her shoes. Fortunately she met a man who also loved to travel, and she snapped him right up. Married for over twenty years, Tina has three wonderful children and has lived in gorgeous places such as Portugal and Brazil.

Living where English reading material was difficult to find had its drawbacks, however. Tina had to come up with creative ways to satisfy her love for romance novels, so she picked up her pen and tried writing one. After her tenth book she realised she was hooked. She was officially a writer.

A three-time 'Golden Heart' finalist, and fluent in Portuguese, Tina now divides her time between the United States and Brazil. She loves to use exotic locales as the backdrop for many of her stories. When she's not writing you can find her either on horseback or soldering stained-glass panels for her home.

Tina loves to hear from readers. You can contact her through her website, or 'friend' her on Facebook.

Recent titles by Tina Beckett:

DOCTOR'S MILE-HIGH FLING
DOCTOR'S GUIDE TO DATING IN THE JUNGLE

**These books are also available in eBook format
from www.millsandboon.co.uk**

CHAPTER ONE

Wɪʏ was he here?

Mark Branson's eyes slid for the hundredth time to the small child standing beside him at the altar, the boy's dark suit and red tie a miniature version of his own. They could almost be father and son.

But they weren't.

His gaze automatically swept to the left, coming to rest on the bridesmaid across the aisle. The woman he'd once planned to marry in this very church, before life had intervened, and she'd married someone else.

And having her child propped against him as they waited for the wedding to begin was pure torture.

'Do you have the rings?'

Mark blinked and switched his attention back to the priest, the man's gold-embroidered robes and matching cape seeming as ancient as the ornate carvings inside the small Russian Orthodox Church. Candles of all shapes and sizes adorned the altar, placed on glittering stands by the people in attendance. The flickering glow added a sense of awe and mystery to the room, and also provided the only source of illumination. The absence of electric lights in the church had always seemed strange to Mark but, then again, he could count on his fingers the number of services he'd attended here.

The last time had been for his father's memorial service. He could still remember his mother's tears. Her grief so misplaced. Mark had never visited the man's grave. Not once.

A throat cleared. 'The rings?' The concern in the priest's tone echoed off the high ceilings. The groom shot him a look, his best friend's brows lifting in question.

Mark cleared his own throat to make sure it came out normal. 'I have them.'

Okay, good. The steady throbbing behind his temples hadn't crept down to his voice box. Digging in his pocket, he located the pair of rings and handed them to the boy, who in turn trudged up the two steps to the top of the platform, giving one to the groom and the other to the bride.

The bride, a relative newcomer to the Aleutians, bent down to hug the child and watched as he skipped back down the steps. She then wrinkled her nose and smiled at her soon-to-be-husband, who gazed back at her with besotted eyes.

Mark barely restrained himself from rolling his own. His buddy had it bad.

Willing the child to go and stand beside his mother, who hadn't met Mark's gaze once since they'd taken their places on the steps at the front of the church, he gave an almost audible sigh of frustration. Because the boy wound up back at his side, leaning against him. The turmoil already raging within his gut turned into a firestorm of the worst kind.

Worse than his years in the military. Worse than what he'd returned home to six months ago.

'Do you, Blake Taylor, take Molly McKinna to be your lawfully wedded wife…'

The voice droned on as a curtain of red slowly rose behind Mark's eyelids. Could this get any worse? When his friend had asked him to be best man, he'd known it was a bad idea.

Churches and weddings?

Not for Mark. Not any more.

He'd become adept at drifting from relationship to relationship, never allowing things to become too serious. Never willing to risk the hurt that came with discovering someone you'd cared about had married someone else—had another man's child. It was his own fault, but he'd had no choice. Not at the time.

'Muster Mark?' The words brought his gaze back down to the boy beside him. 'Are we almost done? I'm thusty.'

The slight lisp sent a half-smile tugging at the corners of his mouth, before he cranked them back down. The child had to be almost six years old. A surge of hope had flashed through him the first time he'd seen the boy. Hope that he had been *his* son. But he had been aboard an aircraft carrier in the Arabian Sea at the time, flying missions to Afghanistan, so there was no chance.

He swallowed the bile that rose in his throat. He'd told her to move on with her life, and she'd done exactly that. Two years after his plane had left Dutch Harbor that final time.

Which brought him back to his original question. *Why was he here?*

A question that had nothing to do with witnessing his best friend's wedding and everything to do with moving back to his hometown. He swore once his dad died, he'd never come back, but his mom had seemed so…

Frail.

Terrified of being alone for the first time in her adult life. So he'd done what he'd tried to do as a young boy, protect her from the bad things in the world. He wasn't any better at it now than he'd been all those years ago.

He glanced down at the kid, who was about the same age Mark had been when he had realized something was terribly wrong with his family. That they were different from the families of his classmates and friends. Hence the fights he'd frequently got into. The need to prove he was tougher—better than them all. It had also kept anyone from focusing on the truth behind his bruises.

Almost against his will, his hand went to the boy's head,

resting for a second on the dark silky hair—so like his mother's. 'A few more minutes,' he whispered, realizing he'd never answered the child's question.

The kid blinked up at him, eyes trusting. Innocent.

Hell, he hoped Sammi knew enough to protect that at all costs.

He glanced over at her again, this time finding her brown eyes staring at him, brows drawn together in worry. He had a feeling if she could snatch her child away from him without causing a scene, she'd do it in a heartbeat.

Mark removed his hand from the boy's head, and crossed his arms over his chest, staring back at her in defiance. She jerked her attention away and faced the bride and the groom, her teeth digging into her soft bottom lip.

Her customary braid was gone today, her long dark hair left free to spill over her bare shoulders and halfway down her back. Thick and glossy, he knew firsthand how decadent those silky strands felt as they flowed across his hands...his body.

He shifted in his spot to keep from remembering too deeply, knowing this was not the time or place. Later, when he slugged back his first shot of whiskey and tried to push away the horrors of the last eight years, he could afford to nurse his regrets.

But he wouldn't go back and change how he'd done things. It had been the right thing to do under the circumstances. The only thing. His father had made sure of that when he'd cracked open the tiny velvet box and discovered Mark's secret.

Well, well, boy. What have we here? The slow, ugly smile that had made Mark's insides tighten with dread had appeared. *Don't worry. I'll make sure the girlie is given a proper Branson welcome.*

He'd left for Anchorage the next day, the engagement ring tucked into the pocket of his jeans, a duffle bag slung over his shoulder. He'd shown up at the first recruitment station he could find...and the rest was history.

Soft clapping around him made him realize the bride and

groom were now in each other's arms, their lips locked together.

He couldn't bring himself to applaud, so he dropped his hands to his sides. When his gaze wandered back to Sammi, he noted that she was standing as still as a stone, her knuckles showing white as she clenched the stems of her bouquet.

How soon could he get out of there?

There was no reception planned, which was a big relief. He didn't have to mingle and make small talk about how great it was that the bride and groom had finally gotten hitched. Or how wonderful it was that they were moving permanently to Anchorage. Mark had never thought his buddy, of all people, would ever leave the island.

Love conquers all.

Wrong.

Sometimes love just turned you into a victim.

His friend's desertion, though, meant it was now Sammi… and him…doing the island's medevacs. Why he'd agreed to take the job, he had no idea. He should have said no, that he was strictly a tourist pilot, sticking to a fluffy job that required nothing more than a smile and a canned speech. Nothing like the life-and-death missions he'd flown in the military—or the terrible images that still invaded his thoughts and woke him in the night. But it was either that or stand in the way of his buddy's happiness.

And his friend knew how to lay on the guilt. He always had.

The pair at the front of the church broke apart amidst laughter. They pivoted towards the small assembly and started down the aisle to the pipe organ's piercing rendition of the 'Hallelujah Chorus', drawing more chuckles from friends and family. The groom put his arms around his bride and pulled her close, stopping for another kiss before they'd gone a half-dozen steps.

All Mark wanted to do was escape.

The rest of the wedding party—he, Sammi, and Sammi's son—turned to follow suit. He started to hold out his elbow for

Sammi as he'd been instructed by his friend—under threat of death—but found her boy's fingers grabbing his hand instead.

Sammi shot him a glare that could have scalded milk and swept in front of him, perfectly rounded curves showcased by her snug emerald dress. The thing actually shimmered with each angry swish of her hips. It took several seconds and a tug at his hand before he realized he was still standing there, rooted in place, as Sammi drew further and further away.

He forced himself to move, having to dial back on the length of his strides to match the kid's. By the time they caught up with her, she was standing in the reception line by the front doors of the church, and he was once again trying to figure out why he was there.

Samantha Grey Trenton sucked down a deep breath and tried not to let her rising panic overwhelm her. Her son Toby's sudden fascination with Mark was nothing more than the fact that he was tall and dark like his father, her ex-husband. Despite the physical resemblance, though, Mark was not the kind of person she wanted her son hanging around. The kind that led you on for as long as it suited him and then left with barely a word.

'I think I have something of yours.' Low and deep, the murmured words slid over her, his breath ruffling her hair.

She swallowed, then turned to face him, realizing with relief he was talking about Toby and not some sentimental relic from the past. That thought caused a warning prickle behind her eyelids that she forced back with a single harsh blink.

Mark's hand came out, her son's small fingers still gripping it like a lamprey. No choice. Her only hope was to try to take possession of him without touching anything but Toby.

Except it ended up being impossible.

In order to take her son's hand, she was forced to wriggle her fingertips between their palms. Mark's warm skin sizzled against her icy flesh, and for a split second all three of their hands were sealed together: Hers, Toby's, and a stranger's.

The prickle reappeared. Oh, God, she was going to lose it. Right here in front of all these people.

The image of the funny, laid-back boy who'd asked her to be his date for their senior prom—whose desperate kisses had awoken something deep inside her—appeared in the back of her mind. But that person was gone for ever, destroyed when he had announced he was going into the military. That shocking decree had come just weeks after he'd professed his love for her, his face turning a charming shade of red as he'd said the words.

It had all been a lie, however. A way to get her into his bed, because there'd been no promise of a future when he'd left. Just a few tight-jawed words spoken at the front door of her house. Then he had gone. The remembered humiliation of that night still had the power to crush her heart in a giant fist.

The tall, rugged man who'd returned to Dutch Harbor eight years later was indeed a stranger. Flippant, arrogant and who now chased anyone in a skirt.

Anyone but her.

With a start, she realized Mark was now eyeing her, their hands still joined together. She gulped and with a quick move, prised Toby's hand free. She moved a few steps forward in line, needing to put some distance between her and Mark.

Please let me get through this in one piece.

That tiny prayer seemed doomed the second she sensed the heat from Mark's body close behind her. Too close.

Ignore him. You've done it for the last six months. You can do it now.

Not so easy this time as Toby had twisted around to look, a contented sigh lifting his thin chest. She listened for the warning wheeze, but it didn't happen. A dose of self-righteous anger whipped up at the deadly charisma her former beau gave off in waves. She would not let him hurt her son the way he'd hurt her.

She leaned down. 'Just a few more minutes.' She realized

too late those were almost the exact words she'd heard Mark whisper to him earlier.

Thank heavens she hadn't waited around for Mark's return. Because he now barely gave her the time of day. And she wasn't much better. She avoided him whenever she could—not an easy feat on an island like Dutch Harbor—and the only times he'd appeared at the clinic over these last months had been to deliver a tourist who'd gotten a scrape or a bruise.

Her turn to offer her congratulations to the happy couple. *Finally!*

She pasted on a smile as she reached out her free hand to Blake, the groom. 'So you went and did it.' She tried to keep her voice light, but it betrayed her by shaking just the tiniest bit. She pushed on, anyway. 'I can't believe you're leaving the island and taking Molly with you.' Blake, Mark, and Sammi had joined forces during their childhood days, becoming a kind of mod squad—inseparable and lifelong friends. Those strands were now tattered and worn—she doubted they could ever be woven together again.

Blake laughed, evidently not noticing the strain she was under. 'I think if Molly had a choice, she'd never leave Dutch Harbor.'

Molly had worked as a doctor at the tiny clinic with Sammi for the last year until her funding had dried up, forcing her to move back to Anchorage. She and Blake had met while doing medevacs and, after a rocky start, realized they were meant for each other. Once she left, Sammi would be stuck doing medical evacuations with Mark, not something she was looking forward to.

Who was she kidding? She was dreading it.

Pausing to gather her thoughts, she tried to keep her mind on the happy couple and off her own problems. 'Treat her right, Blake. Or I'll come and find you.'

'I intend to.'

While Blake squatted to talk to Toby, Sammi moved over to embrace the bride. 'Be happy,' she whispered.

'You too.'

If only it were that easy.

She sensed Blake rise to his feet to greet Mark. At the sound of awkward male hugs—complete with palms delivering a few resounding smacks to the other's back—she had to fight back a smile.

She tried to tune out their words, but Mark's 'You caved, bro' caught her attention, the wry tone as flip as ever.

The bride's voice brought her back to the present. 'Okay, you two, I'm tired and starving.' She crinkled her nose. 'And I still have a three-hour flight to Anchorage to get through.'

That drew a laugh from Sammi. Her friend had married a pilot, yet she didn't like to fly. At all. Talk about opposites attracting. She gave Molly another quick hug. 'You'll be fine.'

Molly smiled. 'I know I will. I just like the extra handholding it gets me.'

Those words made Sammi's heart ache. Although she was over the moon that her two friends had found each other, she was sad she'd never found that same perfect happiness. Her ex-husband had done his best, but in the end they'd both known it wasn't meant to be. When Toby had been one, they'd separated. They'd finalized their divorce two weeks before Toby's second birthday. Her ex, now living in Anchorage, had remarried and was, to all appearances, blissfully happy with his second wife. Even Toby liked her.

A throat cleared behind her, making her jump. She realized she was holding up the line and that Mark couldn't get around her in the narrow gap between the door and the newly married couple without touching her. Again. The thought made her quake inside. She squeaked out a quick 'Sorry'.

Then she grabbed Toby's hand and did the only thing she could think of.

She fled.

CHAPTER TWO

SAMMI pumped the inhaler twice and waited.

Toby, still half-asleep, lay on his back propped in a nest of pillows. The terrifying rattle in his chest slowly eased as the albuterol flooded his lungs, widening his breathing passages to allow more air flow.

As Community Health Aide for the island, she knew better than to panic, but when it was your own son… She closed her eyes. Who could maintain any kind of objectivity under those circumstances?

Not that she had much of that anyway. Molly had continually fussed at her for rushing from one house to another to check on patients she'd just seen the day before.

'You're going to wear yourself out this way' had been the rebuke *du jour*.

Her friend was right, but she hadn't been able to stop.

Now that Molly was gone and with only one other physician's assistant on staff at the clinic, she wouldn't have the luxury of taking off at any hour of day to check on her patients. And either she or the PA would now have to accompany any medevac flights headed to Anchorage. The good part was that she'd be able to meet up with Molly periodically. The bad part was that she was stuck flying with Mark—although Blake could still handle cases that weren't life or death and who could wait the three hours it took him to reach Dutch Harbor.

'Better?' she asked her son, his breathing now almost back to normal.

He nodded sleepily, trying to squinch his way back into his cocoon of warm covers.

'Not so fast, bud. Let's just wait another minute or two.'

His impatient sigh made her smile. Okay, if he could do that, instead of gasping for each breath, she could afford to let him go back to sleep. She tucked him in and stood over his bed, watching him for a second. Before putting the inhaler back on the book-packed nightstand beside his bed, she shook it to see how much of the medicine remained.

Were they going through it faster than normal?

She couldn't shake the feeling that Toby's attacks were coming more frequently than in the past.

Checking the child monitor before she clicked the lights off, she headed back to her own room, hoping she could squeeze her eyelids shut long enough to turn off her brain. She needed the sleep, or tomorrow promised to be a long, exhausting day.

'Mrs. Litchfield is in room one. One of her joints is swollen to almost twice its size.' The receptionist handed Sammi a file folder.

She tossed her braid over her shoulder, catching a movement outside the front plate-glass window as she did.

Mark. He was striding by on his way to the airport, hands stuffed into the front pockets of his leather bomber jacket, long, loose limbs moving in a way that drew the eye. Not quite a swagger, his stride gave off an air of easy confidence that said he didn't care what the world thought of him.

And unlike Sammi, who couldn't seem to look away, the man didn't spare a glance at the clinic, or at her. With a sigh, she forced herself to turn away and head to the exam room.

As soon as she arrived, all thoughts of Mark evaporated when Barbara Litchfield, a woman in her mid-fifties, climbed to her feet and greeted her.

'Sorry to come back so soon,' she said, the regret in her voice unmistakable.

'What are you talking about? I told you to get back in here at the first hint of trouble. Arthritis is nothing to play around with. I know you need those fingers whole and strong.'

A retired orchestral pianist, Barbara had moved to the Aleutians with her husband when he'd retired from a corporate job a couple of years ago. At a time when most retirees sought refuge in the south, hoping for warm, sunny days of golfing and fun, the Litchfields had bucked the trend, fitting right into the harsh landscape of Dutch Harbor. Barbara taught piano lessons—free of charge—to a few of the local kids. It meant a lot to both the former pianist and the kids she worked with. Those fingers were important, and not just for her physical health.

Sammi snapped on a pair of gloves. 'Let's take a look, shall we?'

Taking the other woman's hands in hers, she spotted the affected joint immediately. Swollen and angry red, her left ring finger didn't look happy, and for good reason. Molly frowned when she noted the woman's wedding band. 'Why is that still on?'

'I tried to get it off this morning when I realized how bad it was, but it wouldn't budge, and when I tried to force it…' Her voice trailed away.

'It's okay. The base of your finger isn't swollen at the moment, but if it begins to swell, we may need to cut the ring off.' She put a hand on the other woman's shoulder. 'We won't unless it's absolutely necessary, okay? In the meantime, I'm going to give you a shot of cortisone in the joint. Then I really want you to see a rheumatologist in Anchorage. I'll make a phone call and get you in as soon as possible.'

'I can't just keep taking Advil?'

Sammy shook her head. 'That used to be how we treated arthritis, thinking if we could get the inflammation under control, we could preserve the joint. But newer research suggests the real damage happens much earlier in the disease, even before it shows up on X-rays.'

Just like the damage to Sammi and Mark's relationship. Just as their feelings for each other started to gain a foothold, unseen currents swirled around them, eating away at the foundation. By the time she'd realized just how deeply she'd fallen for him, the mysterious corrosive agent had done its job. The silver cord joining them had snapped and Mark had bolted.

So why did seeing him walk down the street this morning still tug at something inside her? And why had seeing her son's hand enveloped in his at the wedding a week ago turned her heart inside out?

She shook off the questions. It didn't matter. She'd gotten married, had a child with someone else. Mark had dated plenty of other women since his return.

There was nothing between them any more.

'Let me make a quick phone call then I'll give you the injection.' Sammi scribbled a couple of notes down on the chart. 'I'll be right back.'

The phone call took less than five minutes. A bit of arm twisting on her end, the promise of a jar of home-made salmonberry jam when the season rolled around, and Barbara had her appointment. Two weeks from today, record time for that kind of specialist. But she and Chris Masters went way back. One of the few islanders who'd gone to medical school and left the Aleutians, he was now a highly sought-after rheumatologist. Appointments with him could take months.

Satisfied, she made a note to herself that her debt to fellow doctors was now up to ten pints of jam and a pie. Not to mention her son, who'd made her promise on her life not to give all their jelly away again this year.

Speaking of Toby...

She jogged back to the reception area. 'What time is it?'

Lynn's raised brows told her even before she spoke. 'Two o'clock, and you've missed lunch again.'

'Right. I'll eat as soon as I'm done with Mrs. Litchfield.
Promise.'

'You'd better. I've already locked the front door, just in case.'

Sammi laughed. 'Thanks.'

'I'm going to start heating your food in the microwave, so
don't take long.' She paused. 'I'm heating mine too.'

In other words, if Sammi delayed, her receptionist would
also go hungry. 'I'll be there by the time you pour the coffee.'

The injection was given and Sammi unlatched the front door
to let Barbara out—a sheaf of papers and instructions clutched
in her hands. She pushed the door closed again, twisting her
head around when Lynn's threat reached her ears. 'Coffee's
going into the mugs.'

'I'll be right—'

The front door started to blow open, probably a result of the
gusty conditions today. Sammi was leaning her entire weight
onto it to force it shut when a harsh yelp, a colorful string of
words and something squishy stopped her in her tracks.

Eyes wide, she turned to look. The doorway she'd sworn
was empty a second ago was now filled with Mark, and that
squishy thing…

Yikes, she'd just crunched his hand in the door!

'Coffee's getting cold.' Lynn's warning was drowned by the
realization of what she'd just done.

She jerked the door wide. 'Oh, God, Mark. I'm sorry. I had
no idea you were there. Or I'd have never…'

'Never what? Slammed the door on me?' He shook his injured hand, the graveled accusation bringing back the fact that
she'd done exactly that once upon a time. When he'd announced
his intention of moving away to join the armed forces, she'd
slammed the door in his face with a 'Don't bother coming by
before you leave'.

But that was all in the past, where it would stay.

'Come in so I can look at that hand.'

'It's fine.'

'Seriously. It could be broken.'

He gave a wry laugh. 'You really think I'd let you set it if it were? I'd probably end up with permanently crooked fingers.'

'I can think of at least one finger I'd like to fix permanently.' The one he showed to the world. Not a visible gesture, but one he exuded with his attitude.

In answer to her statement, he laughed. A genuine chuckle that moved from his stomach to his mouth…to his gorgeous green eyes. It took her breath away, and she had to force herself not to gasp.

'I'm not *that* bad, am I?' His brows went up.

Worse. The word came and went without her uttering a single sound.

Before she could give him an actual answer, Lynn peeked out from the other room, her mouth rounding in a perfect 'O' as she realized who was standing there. She'd grown up on the island, knew about Sammi and Mark's infamous past.

'You're going to have to start without me,' Sammi said. 'Mark's gotten an…injury that should probably be checked out.'

Mark grinned in the receptionist's direction and the woman's color immediately deepened to an ill-looking salmon, before she nodded and withdrew.

Damn him. How could he have that effect on every woman he encountered? And why had she been so stupid to fall for it herself all those years ago? Well, no danger of that now. She'd found a cure, and that was her son. She'd protect him from being hurt at all costs. And Mark could do exactly that with very little effort.

Jaw tight, she led the way to one of the exam rooms. 'Hop up on the table.'

He leaned against it instead. 'Don't I get a gown?'

'Don't push your luck.' Despite her irritation, the man still had the power to make her lips curve from the inside out. She pressed them together so he wouldn't see as she started toward the dispenser on the wall.

Gloves? Really?

Yes.

Wearing them would give her a measure of protection that had nothing to do with disease and everything to do with self-preservation. She glanced into his face. Would he know the reason?

Yep. It was there in the brow that lifted a quarter of a centimeter.

Forget it. She wouldn't let him know how terrified she was of touching him or how taking her son's hand from his had twisted her heart and left it raw and vulnerable.

She stopped in front of him and tilted her head to meet his gaze. 'Where does it hurt?'

'Seriously?'

'No more games, Mark. You could have broken something.'

His cocky smile disappeared and something dark and scary passed through his eyes. 'Did I, Sam? Break something?'

For the longest moment she couldn't breathe, couldn't tear her gaze from his. No one ever called her Sam.

No one, except Mark.

And she had the distinct impression the broken thing he was asking about had nothing to do with his hand and everything to do with her. No, that couldn't be right. He hadn't cared one iota about the damage he'd caused when he'd taken off without so much as a 'Why?'.

She shook her head, but had to avert her eyes as she did. 'Let me see your hand.'

He held it out, and she winced at the long diagonal stripe of discoloration already showing up just below his metacarpo-phalangeal joints. He must have had his hand wrapped around the frame of the door when she'd leaned against it. 'Wiggle your fingers.'

He obliged, and Sammi watched for a reaction as he curled his fingers into a loose fist and released them. Only there was no reaction. 'It doesn't hurt?'

'It was slammed in a door. What do you think?'

The amused sarcasm was back in place. She decided not to rise to the bait this time. 'Palm up.'

It was only when he turned his hand over that she realized she was avoiding touching him. But she was going to have to eventually. She'd have to X-ray his hand at the very least.

Suck it up, Sammi.

Sliding her fingertips beneath the back of his hand and desperately wishing she'd gone for the gloves after all, she tested the swelling on his palm with her thumb. 'I don't think anything is broken, but I do want to take an X-ray.'

She glanced up, surprised to find a muscle tic in his jaw. 'That bad?' she asked.

'You have no idea.'

'Hmm…' She looked closer at his hand, turning it gently. Maybe there was more damage than she'd thought. 'Follow me.'

Leading him into the tiny X-ray room, she fitted him with a lead apron, forbidding herself from thinking about exactly what she was protecting. She lined up his hand on the table and used the flexible arm on the X-ray tube to pull it down over the injured area, glad to be able to keep her mind on the job. 'I should be able to get this all on one frame, but if not, we'll take a couple more. Hold still for a second.'

She went into the control booth and took the first film, then rejoined him, swinging the tube away from his hand. 'All done. Let's see what we've got.' A thought occurred to her as she pressed buttons on the computer to call up the image. 'Why did you come to the clinic anyway? Are you sick?'

The correct X-ray flashed up, and Sammi zeroed in on the injured portion, not seeing any obvious breaks. Before she could heave a sigh of relief, though, several areas of calcification on his middle phalanges caught her attention. Fractures. Each apparently healed and running across his hand in a line. If not for the location of the bruise from where she'd slammed the door, Sammi would swear she was looking at his current injury. Except these were old. Already fused together.

As she stared, trying to work out how he could have broken a succession of bones like that, Mark's voice came through. 'I'm not sick. I came by to tell you I'm…'

His voice faded away as her eyes met his, horrified realization sweeping through her chest. 'Oh, my God, Mark. Did your father do this to you?'

CHAPTER THREE

IT TOOK a second or two for Sammi's words to filter through his head and another few to register the horror in her eyes. How had she…?

His gaze went to the X-ray still displayed on the computer screen, and he knew what she'd seen. Hell, the days of his father's anger were long gone, replaced by things that were a whole lot worse. And the last thing he wanted now was her—or anyone's—pity. 'Is the damn thing broken or not?'

'Not this time, but—'

'That's all I needed to hear.' He did *not* want to relive the moment when reining in his temper—and being too stubborn to run—had resulted in a steel-toed boot crunching down on his hand, snapping four of the teenage bones with little effort. Sammi had asked about his father once in high school, and he'd blown her off—just like he had everyone. 'As I was saying, I came by because I'm flying some customers back to Anchorage this afternoon. I thought I'd see if the clinic needed me to pick up any supplies from Alaska Regional while I'm there. I didn't realize… I thought today was Hannah's day to work.'

He swore at himself the second the words had left his mouth. There was no reason to let her know he'd been avoiding her or that the need to stay as far away from her as possible had grown since enduring Blake's wedding. He'd caught a glimpse of what his life could've been like had things been different. If he'd given Sammi that ring.

But he hadn't.

So he'd keep doing what had worked for him over the past eight years: put one foot in front of the other. No reason to think it wouldn't keep on working. In fact, he was due for his weekly trip to the local watering hole. Since he was going to Anchorage anyway, he could kill two birds with one stone. And hopefully stave off the nightmares, which had come back with a vengeance after holding Toby's hand that evening in church.

'Hannah went to Akutan for the day. I offered to fill in for her.' Sammi's words were accompanied by a tilt of her chin, but he could swear a tiny glimmer of hurt appeared in her eyes before it winked back out.

He swore silently. This was exactly why he needed to stay away from her at all costs. She could knot his insides into a big ball of guilt without even trying. 'Right. So, can you think of anything you—the clinic, that is—needs?'

She stood to her feet. 'Nope. I—*and* the clinic—have everything we could possibly need.'

Well, that certainly put him in his place. Sammi had just let him know, in no uncertain terms, that the *last* thing she needed was him.

The state ferry chugged through the dark waters of the Gulf of Alaska, the rumble of its engines sending subtle vibrations along the length of the vessel. The noise was familiar, comforting. She'd made the trip from Unalaska to Anchorage hundreds of times over the years—the intricate tangle of the Alaska Marine Highway routes burned into her subconscious.

Elbows propped against the railing, Sammi glanced down at Toby. 'Are you cold?' Worried that the chilled air might irritate his bronchial tubes, her gloved hand went to the pocket of her down jacket for the hundredth time, making sure the precious inhaler was within close reach. It was one of the reasons she always reserved a cabin onboard for the two-day trip—despite the extra cost—rather than pitch a tent on the deck like other travelers often did. Especially as the summer air gave way to the frigid gusts of late fall.

'I like being out here.' Toby's words were muffled by the scarf Sammi had draped across his nose and mouth in an effort to keep the air as warm as possible.

The trip to see Toby's father was one she always dreaded. Not only because she hated to be away from her son but because the trip meant she wouldn't have access to her clinic or a hospital during the time it took to get from one place to the other. And flying was an expense she couldn't afford. Toby's father was footing the bill for the trip by water as it was.

You could have asked Mark to take you.

Right. After he'd stalked from the clinic two weeks ago?

She had been wrong to bring up his father, but the words had flown from her mouth before she'd been able to stop them. She doubted many people knew what he'd gone through as a kid, and he'd never openly admitted it to anyone. Even when they'd been together, Mark had avoided talking about his dad. But she'd seen little clues here and there, and she knew in her heart of hearts her hunch was right.

But to say the words out loud...

She cringed. If things between them had been bad before her outburst, they were a hundred times worse now.

The figurative arctic freeze they'd retreated into was more palpable than the real thing—on the open deck of the ferry. If anyone was going to break that frosty silence, it would be him. Not that there was much of a chance of cracking through all those layers without some kind of major thaw. And after more than eight years of icy accumulation, Sammi didn't see that happening.

Her thoughts went back to the X-ray and her initial horror at seeing those old breaks. Once the shock had faded, though, her brain had clicked into gear and worked through some other possibilities. He could have broken his hand in any number of ways. Like having it slammed in a door in a similar fashion to what had happened at the clinic. Only she would have expected one bone to have cracked in that case. Not four. The X-ray she'd taken had been merely a precaution.

Had he gotten them as a result of his military service? Because he hadn't come to the clinic with any injuries since he'd returned to Dutch Harbor—and she didn't remember seeing a cast on him during that time.

He'd never spoken of those years in the navy to anyone on the island, or word would have gotten back to her. Surely Blake knew something. They'd served in the military at the same time. But Blake seemed just as close-mouthed about that period in his life as Mark did. They'd both been pilots in Afghanistan, dangerous work, but Mark had never once bragged, even to impress any of the local girls, which shocked her. She couldn't think of a better way to pick up women than to present yourself as a bad-boy hero who thrived on danger.

In fact, he didn't mention his past at all, something she found a little strange, now that she thought about it. She'd talked about the stuff that had happened in her life on a regular basis, from cute childhood moments to embarrassing tales of teen stupidity. Even her father's history of running around on her mother was common knowledge on the island, much to her mom's keen embarrassment.

'Will it be snowing at the zoo?'

Sammi's mind switched back to the present, and she smiled down at her son, her heart swelling with love. 'I hope not.' Doubly so because Toby's father had always seemed slightly irritated at the limitations placed on their son due to his asthma. A die-hard sports fan, Brad often hinted that Toby's condition wouldn't be as bad if Sammi didn't coddle him so much.

But she didn't. At least, she didn't think she did. What else was she supposed to do when he was gasping and wheezing for breath? Tell him to 'man up' and deal with it?

It was another reason she'd always accompanied Toby on these trips, rather than just ask Brad to come to the island and pick him up. It's not like her ex didn't have the money to fly over for their bi-weekly visits. Neither did she begrudge Toby the time with his father. Brad was a good man, and a decent father—at least he'd never begged off having Toby come and see him—but Sammi also wanted to be somewhere close, in case something went terribly wrong. So she'd sit in a hotel room all day while Brad, along with his new wife and daughter, took Toby on their usual one-day jaunt. She'd stare at her cellphone and will it not to ring. But Toby had always been dropped off at the end of the day healthy, happy, and singularly untraumatized. He never knew his mother went to hell and back until he was delivered safely into her care once again.

At least she and Molly—who'd come back from her honeymoon a week ago—could go out and enjoy a meal. If her friend was off duty for the day. And if she could drag herself away from Blake long enough for them to get in some girl time.

'There it is, Mom!'

Sure enough, off in the distance was a pinpoint strip of land that could only signal they were getting close to docking. 'Do you have all your stuff?'

Toby glanced down at his wheeled backpack. 'I think so. I'm coming back to the hotel room tonight, right? Or am I staying with Daddy?'

'Nope. It's you and me, popcorn and a movie.' She tucked the tail of his scarf into his coat a little better. 'What do you want to see?'

'How about something scary? With zombies and stuff.'

Her brows went up. 'Try again. This time come down a couple of ratings to something within the PG range.'

'Awww, Mom…'

It was a familiar fight, but Sammi wasn't irritated. She knew it was part of Toby's search for independence, but she also knew that at six, he still needed limits. Lots of them. She could be his friend when he was an adult. Until then, she was fully prepared to be the bad guy.

'Hmm… How about that penguin movie you love so much?'

'We've seen that like six thousand times.'

'That's a lot. I had no idea.' She gave him a mock roll of her eyes. 'We can decide once you get back to the hotel, then.'

The next half-hour was spent making sure they weren't forgetting anything on board before the ferry drew up at the docking. When Toby acted like he was going to bolt toward the exit, she took his arm. 'Wait.' She didn't particularly want to be trampled on the way out. So they hung back, allowing the bulk of the passengers to disembark before making their own getaway.

Brad and his family met them in the parking area. There were so many people around that they didn't have to worry about making small talk or about whether or not Sammi should invite them inside her hotel room. She wanted to keep things as cordial as possible, for Toby's sake.

A small pang of envy went through her as Brad bent down and wrapped his son in a big hug. His wife also knelt to say hello, their four-year-old daughter holding tightly to her hand. Sammi wanted to dislike the woman, especially since they'd started their own family almost before the ink had been dry on the divorce papers, but she couldn't. Maribel had never been anything but nice to her, and she seemed to really like Toby. That was all that mattered. That her son was happy and well taken care of.

Brad stood, keeping hold of Toby's hand. 'Do you want to do this like we usually do? We can bring him to the hotel room around eight or nine?'

Something about the way he said it made Sammi fidget. Yes, that was their normal arrangement, so it wasn't like she could suddenly say Toby couldn't go. She just had a funny feeling. The weather had been iffy for the two-day trip on the ferry, but nothing in the forecast seemed to predict anything unusual for a day in mid-October. 'That sounds fine.'

No one asked which hotel, because she always stayed at the same place. And she was always alone when they arrived.

Alone. What an awful-sounding word.

Maybe she needed to put herself back on the market. Toby was growing up quickly. And Brad seemed to have gone on with his life. So why hadn't she?

Certainly not because she was still in love with Brad. She'd been fond of him—had convinced herself he was the stable, steady presence she craved in a husband. Not like her father or Mark who had been there one minute and gone the next. But, in the end, stable and steady hadn't been enough to make the marriage work.

She leaned down and kissed Toby, making sure his back-pack was zipped up tight. 'I guess you're all set.'

'Ready for the zoo?' Brad asked his wife and daughter. Little squeals went up from both the girls, while Toby stood motionless.

Strange. A little while ago he'd been excited about the prospect of being with his dad. Maybe he'd sensed her mood, which he seemed to have an uncanny knack of doing. She hoped not. The last thing she wanted to do was spoil his outing.

'Oh, wait.' Lord, she couldn't believe she'd almost forgotten. Reaching into her jacket pocket, she pulled out Toby's inhaler and handed it to her ex. The skin between Brad's brows puckered a bit, but he said nothing. Instead, he shoved the small canister into the pocket of his own jacket. Her trepidation grew. Brad wouldn't let anything bad happen to Toby. He was *his* son as well. And they'd been through this same routine for the last four years without a hint of trouble.

They turned to go, and Sammi waved them off with a smile that she hoped hid the kernel of sadness that appeared whenever she watched her son walk away from her. She then trudged over to the car rental place, anxious to get to the hotel and kick back and relax.

Right. Kick back and mope was more like it.

Lucky for her, Molly was home when she called and was currently husbandless, since Blake was off on a flight. Maybe today wouldn't be as bad as she feared. Molly swung by the hotel and picked Sammi up, refusing to let her drive all the way out to the house.

'It was on the way to the restaurant,' her friend insisted, once they sat at the table of a popular seafood place.

The aroma of garlic and fresh fish swirled around the foyer, and Sammi gave an appreciative sniff, beginning to relax a little. 'It's been a while since I've been out to eat.'

It was true. Normally on these jaunts she simply grabbed some Chinese takeout and carried it back to the room, as it felt pathetic to sit at a table all by herself. But with Molly there, things seemed a little more festive, a little less sad.

Once they were seated, she cracked open the menu and tried not to wince at the prices. Maybe this was why she didn't go out to eat that much. But she'd earned this respite. Toby was safe, and she wouldn't get that many chances to see Molly now that she was back in Anchorage. 'How's Blake?'

'He's fine. In fact, he's more than fine.' Molly leaned forward, her glance darting around the room before coming back to rest on Sammi with a smile. 'Okay, so we weren't going to tell anyone yet, but...I'm pregnant.'

'What?' So this was why her friend had been practically glowing when she'd arrived at the hotel. 'Holy cow. Are you serious?'

'I am. You wouldn't believe how hard it was to squeeze into my wedding gown.' She laughed. 'But you have to promise not to tell anyone. Blake and I wanted to announce it together once the pregnancy was further along. But you're so far away...and I wanted you to be the first to know.'

Sammi's eyes pricked unexpectedly, remembering her own

excitement when she'd discovered she was pregnant with Toby. 'Oh, Molly, I'm so happy for you. You're going to make a wonderful mother.'

'You think so? I wasn't actually sure I wanted to have children, but...' She laid her menu down. 'Here we are.'

'You're going to love it. Having Toby changed my life. For the better,' she was quick to add. 'You'll be exhausted and frustrated and scared...and you'll love every second of it.'

Molly reached over and squeezed her hand. 'Thank you. I may be calling you for advice at some point.'

The waiter came and took their order, leaving them to chat. About halfway through the meal, Blake strode into the restaurant, his eyes fastening immediately on Molly, who bit her lip and stood as he reached them. 'I thought you said you'd be gone until tomorrow.'

He grinned and dropped a kiss on her mouth, then hugged Sammi. Pulling up a chair next to his wife's, he looped an arm around her shoulders. 'I missed you and decided to come back early. So what have you girls been talking about?'

Molly's cheeks immediately turned pink, causing Blake to lean back in his chair, brows raised. 'I thought so.'

'I know we decided not to tell anyone, but...Sammi is family.'

Blake's mouth quirked. 'Yeah, kind of like an annoying little sister.'

Sammi, although the same age as Blake, had been the runt of the class during their childhood days. He'd never let her forget it, even though she was now five feet seven.

Sammi leaned across the table and swatted his arm. 'Molly doesn't seem to think so.' She paused, letting her eyes convey her true thoughts. 'Seriously, though. Congratulations.'

'Thanks.'

Molly smiled up at him. 'Do you want to order something?'

He plucked a huge battered shrimp from her plate, munching it before he answered. 'No, I ate on the way. I'm stuffed.'

'I can tell,' she said, when he snagged a second piece.

He laughed. 'I'm meeting a friend for drinks later, anyway, so I can't stay. I just wanted to see you first.'

'I see. And just who is this friend?'

Sammi's phone buzzed, indicating she was getting a text. She scrunched her nose. 'Sorry guys, I know it's not polite, but I told Brad to let me know if their plans were going to change. Do you mind?'

'It's fine.' Molly waved her fork.

Retrieving the phone from her handbag, she pressed a button to retrieve the message. The low lighting in the restaurant caused her to squint as she tried to make out the letters, but once she did, she gasped, her heart dropping. 'Oh, God, I have to go.' She threw her napkin on the table and stood.

Alarmed, her friends got to their feet as well. 'What is it?'

She stuffed her phone back in her purse. Her voice shook as she tried to get the words out. 'They're rushing Toby to the hospital.'

CHAPTER FOUR

SAMMI raced through the doors of the emergency room, while Molly parked the car. They'd left Blake at the restaurant to pay the bill and follow in his own vehicle.

Brad met her in the reception area, his wife and daughter nowhere to be seen. 'Where is he?' she demanded, her breath rushing from her lungs.

'Calm down. He's with one of the doctors.'

'Then why the hell are you out here, instead of back there with him?' Toby had to be frightened out of his wits.

Her ex's eyes narrowed in warning. 'I did go with him. But I didn't want you to hear what happened from some stranger.'

'Sorry.' Her anger deflated. 'Was it his asthma?'

'Yes.' He stuffed his hands into his pockets. 'He's never had an attack while with us. I thought it wasn't really that serious…that he'd be okay.'

She remembered his face when she'd handed over the inhaler. He'd thought she was just babying Toby yet again. 'You left his medicine in the car, didn't you?'

'Not on purpose. I had it in my pocket when we left, then asked Toby to put it in his backpack for safekeeping. When we got to the zoo…well, I didn't want him lugging the pack with him all day.'

'I'm going back there to see him.'

By that time, Molly had joined them. 'I'll see where he is.'

'Why didn't you just go and get his inhaler once you realized he was having trouble?'

'It came on so fast. He couldn't get enough air.' His lips tightened. 'I didn't know how long it would take to work. I—I panicked, Sammi.'

She touched his arm, compassion sweeping over her. She knew how frightening Toby's attacks could be. 'You did the right thing getting him here as fast as possible.'

Molly returned. 'He's okay. I'll take you back to him.'

'Thank you.' She glanced at Brad. 'Are you coming?'

'I'll wait for Maribel. She's dropping Jessie off at the sitter's.'

Molly led her back to an exam room, where her son sat on a table holding a nebulizer mask over his mouth and nose. Hurrying over to him, she leaned down and looked into his face. She raised her brows in the wordless question they'd devised to communicate during these times. He answered with a thumbs-up sign, although his breathing still sounded a little ragged to her ears. His color looked good, so Brad had told the truth about not wasting any time getting him here. She pressed her lips to his forehead, then checked the amount of medication remaining in the nebulizer cup. The treatment was about half-finished.

'Did you talk to the doctor?' She glanced at Molly, who was standing by the door.

Molly nodded. 'It was serious…' she glanced toward Toby as if unsure how much to say in front of him '…but manageable. They want to observe him for a couple of hours before they discharge him. They've got a call in to the pulmonologist, who should be here in a few minutes.'

'I—I don't know if Brad still has his inhaler. Can I get a new prescription just in case?'

'I'm sure we've got some extras here at the hospital. I'll give you one to take home with you. Albuterol, right?'

'Yes.' Sammi hopped up onto the bed beside Toby and put

her arms around him, a surge of love and thankfulness going through her. She kissed the top of his head. 'I'm going to leave in a minute or two to give Daddy a chance to see you, okay? He's pretty worried.'

Toby pulled the mask down. 'I want to go home.'

'We will.' She put her hand over his, steering the mask back into place. 'As soon as the doctor says it's safe. We've got a long trip ahead of us tomorrow.'

Molly touched her arm and nodded toward the door. 'The doctor's in the hall.'

'I'm going with Aunt Molly for a minute. I'll be right outside that door, if you need me.' She gave him one last kiss and slid off the table.

Going into the hallway with Molly, she was able to speak with the doctor who'd treated her son. He assured her Toby was going to be fine. His breathing was already better, but they wanted to do a pulmonary function test as soon as he finished with the nebulizer.

Sammi smiled. 'That's Toby's favorite part of any hospital visit.' She sighed. 'Actually, that's the *only* part he likes. It's like a challenge to see if he can beat his last set of results.'

'It's my favorite part too.' Dr. Donnelly's kind blue eyes twinkled, helping to reassure her. 'Believe me, I want our buddy in there to ace that test as much as you do.'

'Thanks for everything you've done. I'm going to run and get his father, okay?'

'Of course,' he answered.

Sammi wasn't sure, but she thought she detected a hint of interest in the man's look at her. The doctor was attractive enough, his dark, conservatively cut hair falling neatly over his forehead. Nothing like Mark's slightly shaggy locks that seemed as loose and free as the rest of him.

Why had she thought of him, of all people?

Besides, despite her earlier thoughts about putting herself back on the market, now was not the time. Not with her son sitting in that room fighting for each breath. 'I'll go and get his father.'

She headed for the waiting room. Brad, his back to her, stood at one of the large windows, staring outside. Maribel had arrived and was leaning against him, whispering in his ear. Sammi hesitated before touching his arm. 'You can see him now. He's better.'

'Thank God.' He turned part way around and met her eyes. 'I think I'll keep an extra inhaler or two on hand from now on. Can you help me get them?'

'I think that's a great idea. Molly's going to see if she can find a couple.' She dropped her hand to her side. 'Go ahead. He's waiting for you.'

Brad and his wife walked away, pushing through the double doors that led to the various exam rooms. She stood there for a few moments, her arms wrapped around her waist, trying to convince herself things were going to be all right. It was a losing battle.

'How is he?' The sudden question raised the hair on her neck. Actually, it wasn't the question itself but the familiar voice behind it. Low and mellow, the tone slid over her like warm honey.

Sammi whirled around to find Mark standing there, both hands shoved into the pockets of his jacket. She could have sworn he wasn't there a second ago. 'How—? What are you doing—?'

'I dropped off some clients this afternoon and was supposed to meet up with Blake later for drinks. He called my cell on his way to the hospital.'

So this was the friend Blake had mentioned meeting earlier. 'He did? Why?'

'He wanted to let me know he might be late.' His jaw tightened. 'Don't worry. He wasn't trying to invade your privacy.'

'I didn't think that.'

So what had she thought? That Mark wouldn't care one way

or the other what happened to her or her son? Yep. But trying to explain that in a way that didn't sound bitter—or like she was stuck in some sad version of the past—was impossible. So she decided to answer his original question instead. 'Toby's better. Brad's with him now.'

'I know. I saw him when I came in.'

There'd never been any love lost between the two men, although she wasn't quite sure why. In school they'd all run in different circles. She'd been a geek, while Mark had hung out with the rougher crowd. Brad had been firmly in the jock camp—the all-American-hero type. Her ex had always kind of looked down on Mark when they'd been kids. Maybe Mark had sensed that.

She crossed her arms over her chest. 'Did you see Blake? He should be here by now.'

'He's waiting for Molly in the cafeteria. We decided to cancel our plans.'

Uh-oh. She'd assumed he was killing time until Blake arrived. Maybe she should start looking for an exit. 'Are you going back to the island tomorrow?'

'If Toby is released by then.'

She blinked, not sure what that had to do with anything. 'What do you mean?'

'Are they planning to hold him overnight?'

Was she missing something? 'No, just observe him for a couple more hours to make sure the attack is over.'

'Good. We should be able to leave in the morning, then.'

'We?'

Okay, there was something strange going on. Where exactly were *they* going?

'I'm flying you back to the island.'

'We bought round trip tickets for the ferry, we can...'

The words died in her throat when he took a step closer, brushing back a strand of hair that had come loose from her braid. 'There's no way in hell I'm letting you take that ferry back to the island. Not with Toby sick.'

His fingers were warm against her skin, and she wanted more than anything to lean into his palm, to hand over a tiny portion of her burden. But she didn't dare. Mark had proved he could—and would—walk away without a backward glance. That's not what she wanted for her son. He was already enamored with Mark as it was. Watching him pilot a plane would only make it worse. The thought made her stiffen against his touch. 'We'll be okay.'

'You're right. You will.' His hand dropped to her shoulder. 'Because you're flying back with me. Both of you.'

Driving Toby and Sammi back to the hotel, Mark wasn't quite sure why she'd seemed so averse to flying with him. Being out in that frigid air couldn't be good for Toby's lungs. Not right after an attack that had landed him in the hospital. And especially not after the way she'd angled her face toward his hand for a second as he'd brushed his fingers across her cheek in the emergency room. His breath had caught, memories of her doing that very same thing in the past sweeping over him.

But neither of them were the kids they'd once been. And Sammi evidently had an easier time accepting that than he did, because she'd pulled away. He, on the other hand, had been lost the moment he'd touched her. All he'd wanted to do was press his lips to hers and feel the response that used to set his world on fire.

He'd told Molly and Blake he'd make sure Sammi got back to the hotel, as her rental car was still there. She hadn't seemed very happy about that either, although she'd kept silent. Glancing over at her as she stared out the passenger window, he wondered if he'd done the right thing in demanding she accept his offer. But she couldn't take Toby on that ferry, dammit. Even *she* had to see that.

'You doing okay back there, buddy?' He peered into the rear-view mirror to find Toby leaning against the window in the back, eyes shut, mouth open. A thrill of anxiety went through him, along with a flashing image of a different boy—blood everywhere as the medics worked on the horrific wounds covering his small body. The same child who inhabited many of his current nightmares.

But Toby wasn't that boy. And he wasn't injured, just asleep. Mark forced his hands to ease their grip on the wheel, and thankfully the memory faded away.

He glanced at Sammi to make sure she hadn't noticed anything. 'He's out.'

'I'm sure he's exhausted.' Sammi twisted around in her seat to look, her dark braid looped over her left shoulder. He'd teased her about that long length of hair in high school, tugging on it repeatedly. Those had been during the light times, when they'd just been good friends. Later, when they'd been more than friends, he could remember wrapping that braid around his hand to hold her in place as he kissed her. Or removing the band and unwinding those thick lustrous strands so that they could fall loose and free.

This was a mistake, and he knew it. Being around her and Toby was reawakening the very things he'd tried to wipe from his mind. But he had no choice. It was time he thought about someone other than himself.

He was. He had been. It's why he'd left Dutch Harbor all those years ago.

So why had he moved back to his hometown? Why hadn't he just stayed away?

Because his mother needed him. At least that's what he told himself.

Soon they were parked in front of the hotel's check-in area. 'Which room?'

'Four-oh-two.' Sammi's voice remained soft. 'Thank you, Mark. I know I didn't seem very grateful back at the hospital, but you're right. It's better for Toby if we fly back. We're not taking you away from a customer?'

It wouldn't matter if they were. This was more important than a tourist. 'Nope. I don't have another charter trip on the docket until Tuesday, and that's just a quick little island hop.'

Mark found the room number and pulled up in front of it. 'I'll help you get him inside, then I'll check in. I'll call you with my room number.'

'Wait. Weren't you going to stay with Blake and Molly?' In the dark, he could just make out her frown.

'I thought it might be easier to leave first thing if I stayed here. They're forecasting sleet in the morning, and I'd like to be in the air before it hits.' He hesitated. 'And if something happens, you might need someone nearby.'

His chest tightened at the thought.

She unbuckled her seat belt then shoved her arms through the sleeves of her down jacket. She didn't say anything as she clicked open the door and stepped from the car, so Mark had no idea if she was happy or furious that he was staying at the hotel. It didn't matter either way. It was the right thing to do.

Getting out of the car as well, he pulled Toby's door open and carefully released the latch on the seat belt. Then he slid his arms under the boy's shoulders and knees and eased him from the car, thankful the kid's jacket was still buttoned up tight. He was light. Almost as light as the boy he'd once carried to his chopper. That seemed like a lifetime ago now.

Had it only been a year?

It's over. Done. You can't undo the past.

Mark used his own body to block the wind, backing towards the door that Sammi had already opened.

'He likes the far bed,' she whispered as they went past.

'His backpack is still in the car.' Mark walked toward the bed, glancing down at the child's slack face and dark lashes fanned out against his cheeks. A shard of loss went through his chest, and he suddenly had trouble catching his breath.

After setting the boy down on the blue bedspread, he carefully unzipped his coat, thankful the heat had been left on in the room. The weather conditions had turned frigid outside. So different from the stifling heat of Afghanistan and its twin scents of blood and fear that would often sweep through their camp like a dust storm, coating everything in sight. Even now it stung his nostrils, filled his lungs—

'Mark?'

He jerked upright, turning toward her. 'Yes?'

'I—I wanted to thank you for what you're doing. It means a lot to me.' Before he could prepare himself, she stood on tiptoe and pressed her lips to his cheek. The touch was as light as a feather, but it was as if something in his heart clicked back on. Fear—and something much stronger—began racing through his veins.

He had to take a step back before he wrapped an arm around her waist and dragged her into his arms, hoping her very presence could banish the memories he'd locked deep inside himself. 'Don't worry about it. I'd do the same for anyone.'

Something flared behind her eyes, and he damned himself for not thinking before he opened his big mouth. Yes, he'd do it for anyone, but the suggestion had been so much more than the casual offer from one stranger to another.

As she said goodbye and closed the door on him, he had his first inkling that he might be headed on a dangerous course. He couldn't save the world, he'd already proved that to himself and everyone around him. He'd left Dutch Harbor eight years ago a scared and messed-up kid. He'd returned an even more screwed-up man. One who could barely take care of himself, much less anyone else. He'd do well to keep that in mind before making any other big promises he couldn't keep.

Like promising a little boy he'd be fine? That he wouldn't die like his mother and father had?

Mark set off for the lobby, a wave of exhaustion going through him. If there was one thing he'd learned, it was that promises were the stuff of fairy-tales—not worth more than the hot air used to voice them. He'd broken one too many of them over the course of his life.

But not any more.

He pulled off his clothes and slid beneath the bulky covers of his bed, the chill from the sheets clinging to skin like the ice that sometimes coated the props on his plane.

No more promises from him. Not to Toby. And especially not to Sammi.

Mark frowned as he peered over the steaming surface of the desert. The wind from his chopper's rotors whipped a woman's dark hair around her face as she pushed toward the aircraft. Even from a hundred yards away, something about her looked familiar.

The wife of their translator, who was now dead at the hands of insurgents. His eyes went to the bundle she carried in her arms.

A bomb!

The thought scrabbled through his mind, sending fear spiking through his veins.

The medics had just raced to help several downed soldiers who'd gotten caught in the crossfire, leaving Mark alone.

She moved a few yards closer. Mark motioned for her to stay away that it was too dangerous for her to be here, but she shook her head, taking another step. The swirling currents caused the cloth to fall away from the top portion of the object, allowing Mark to catch a glimpse of what was inside. Instead of a hardwired mass of explosives, a small face appeared, a vicious smear of red across his temple…his cheek.

Ahmed, her child!

Without thinking, he shoved open his door and hopped down to her level, blocking the wind with his body like he'd done with Toby earlier.

No. Toby wasn't here. He was far away.

Before he could reach them, she set the child down, then turned and began running in the opposite direction.

What the hell? Why was she abandoning him?

Mark raced toward the boy, just as a blinding explosion came from the direction of the boy's mother. He fell to his knees as something struck his chest. A piece of shrapnel. His eyes went to the woman, but she was gone, smoke still drifting from the spot where she'd been.

It had been a bomb after all.

The boy! Reaching him, he ripped open the blanket and gasped as large sucking chest wounds met his eyes.

He forced his lips to move, but they did so in slow motion, his voice a garbled distortion of human speech. 'Hang…on… I've…got you.' He picked the bundle up, ignoring the sting in his chest, then he climbed back aboard the plane, setting the child down in the seat next to him. Things went from slow motion to rapid fire as bodies suddenly piled inside the aircraft—mouths gaping, eyes staring—crowding every available inch of space.

Sharp pinging sounds against the metal skin of the chopper let him know they were under attack.

Mark's eyes flew open. He blinked rapidly as he tried to figure out what to do next, where to go as darkness swallowed him whole. The pinging continued, growing louder by the second.

No, not gunfire. Something else.

His chest heaved as he tried to suck down breath after breath and push through his terror.

Something weighed him down, and he kicked out at it, finding the object soft and light—fabric—rather than the heavy, solid mass he expected to encounter. Cold air hit him as the cloth fell away, and a shudder rolled through him. He was drenched with sweat. Naked.

Where was his uniform? His chopper?

Gone. Like the woman and the boy.

He blinked again and his surroundings came into sharp

focus. He was lying in a bed, not face down in blistering sand. No screams. No blood. Just the sound of something hitting the glass windowpane to his left.

Sleet.

Reality swept over him in a rush as his brain clicked back into gear. He was in a hotel room in Anchorage, far from the horror and carnage he'd lived through in Afghanistan.

But the mother and child, although nothing more than figments of his imagination now, had once been living, breathing souls. And the promise he'd made to them both had been snatched away in the space of a few mismatched heartbeats, leaving him cold. Empty.

Carrying nothing, except regret.

CHAPTER FIVE

'COOL! I get to ride on Uncle Mark's plane?'

Uncle? What's with that?

'Yes, so we need to hurry and get ready.' A light dusting of snow had fallen just after midnight, leaving a shimmery coating on the tree branches—almost as if Mother Nature had uncapped a jar of silvery glitter and let the wind sift it across the landscape. The effect this morning, as she peered out the drapes of the hotel room, was gorgeous.

As beautiful as it was, the icy conditions also made her nervous. Mark had mentioned wanting to leave *before* the snow hit. His plane was an amphibian type, so he could land directly on the water if need be, but that wouldn't help them during take-off, as his plane was parked at the Merrill Field airport.

Even as she thought it, she squinted skywards and found it a menacing shade of grey. She could only pray the runway stayed clear a little while longer. And that the weather en route to Dutch Harbor co-operated. She wasn't needed at the clinic today, but she was on the schedule for Monday. She really didn't want to sit around in Anchorage for the next couple of days if conditions turned ugly. Especially since she'd already called the rental car agency this morning and had them pick up the vehicle.

Dropping the curtain, she swung back to her son, assessing his condition. He was lounging on the bed, his attention focused on his handheld game unit—cheeks bright with excitement, breathing normal. You'd never know by looking at him that he'd endured a serious asthma attack less than twelve hours ago.

She double-checked his backpack for his inhaler, removed it and put it inside her own jacket pocket for safekeeping. 'I'll bet your dad is glad you're all better.'

Brad had called first thing that morning to check on Toby. He hadn't wasted any time with chit-chat but had asked to speak with his son. Once reassured that everything was okay, he'd rung off.

'Yep, he is.'

Sammi had just retrieved Toby's coat from the small closet when a knock at the door made her jump. Mark. She glanced at her watch. Right on time, too.

Her son didn't wait for her to make the first move. He leaped from the bed and yanked the door wide open before she could stop him.

She put a hand on his shoulder. 'Hey, remember what we discussed a few weeks ago? Never open the door without checking to see who it is, first. It could be someone who's not very nice.'

'Sorry, Mom.'

Her eyes went to Mark, noting the still damp hair slicked back from his face and just starting to curl slightly at the ends. Toby shrugged away from her and attached himself to the other man's hand.

Mark's lips tightened. 'Your mom is right, bud. It could definitely be someone who's not very nice. It could even be someone like me.'

'But you *are* nice,' said Toby.

Mark's eyes went to hers and stuck there for a moment. 'There are not-so-nice sides to everyone.'

There was a brittle edge to his words that she didn't understand.

Find a safer subject, then.

'How are the conditions out there?'

Or you could always go for the obvious choice and ask about the weather.

Toby let go of him to pull his backpack closer, and she could have sworn Mark's hand gave a subtle swipe against the fabric of his jeans as if wiping away every trace of her son's touch. What could the man possibly have against Toby? He seemed to stiffen up whenever he was around. She shrugged it off. Some people just didn't like kids.

Except he'd offered to fly them to Dutch Harbor to keep him safe.

'We'll make it into the air, if that's what you're asking.' Mark stepped to the side, putting another foot or so of space between him and Toby. 'But we should get going if we want to take off before the worst of it hits.'

'I'm okay with doing whatever it takes to avoid the storm.'

'So am I.'

She blinked. Again, there seemed to be some weird intensity behind the words as if he was talking about something other than the weather. 'Um, did you eat breakfast?'

He shifted his weight. 'Yes. You?'

'I packed some cereal bars before we left home. We'll be fine until we get back.'

'I have some juice and snacks on the plane if you get hungry on the way.'

So she could be beholden to him more than she already was? She didn't think so. 'I've got extras as well.'

They stared at each other for a few more seconds as if performing a delicate dance in which neither one wanted to upset the balance and send the other careening over some unseen edge—or tumble over it themselves.

Toby broke the uneasy silence, peering into his backpack. 'Mom, I can't find my inhaler.' The slight panic in his voice brought her attention fully back to him, her heart cramping.

No six-year-old should have to worry about whether or not he'd be able to take his next breath.

Pulling the small canister out of her pocket, she held it up. 'I have it. Sorry.' *Wait, was he okay?* 'Do you need it? *Please, God, no.*

He shook his head. 'I just didn't want to not have it like...'

Like yesterday. Her chest tightened further. His pediatrician said there was a good chance he'd outgrow some of his breathing problems—some children did. She could only hope Toby was one of the lucky ones.

Mark nudged the curtain aside to glance out the window. 'Are we ready, then? The sky's getting darker.'

'I think so.' She made a quick sweep of the room, zeroing in on Toby's hand-held game system, which he'd tossed on the bed in order to answer the door. 'Um, missing something, Tobe?'

'Oh, yeah.' He gave her a sheepish grin as he went over to retrieve it. 'But I did check on my medicine.'

'You did. And I appreciate you taking responsibility for it.' She reached for her overnight case, only to have Mark take it from her. He then picked up Toby's backpack as well, holding it out so her son could stuff the game system inside one of the back zippered compartments.

They made it to the airport in record time, and Mark filed their flight plan. When he opened the plane, Toby scrambled up, heading straight for the copilot seat, but Mark stopped him. 'I think it's safer for you to buckle up in that seat right over there.' He pointed to the chair directly behind the pilot's seat. 'It's got a really great view.'

Toby groaned in disappointment, but plopped down into the seat indicated, pulling his game out of his backpack and plugging in his earbuds.

So much for the view. Surely once they took off, Toby would lose interest in his game and enjoy his first flight.

Sammi took a moment to look around. She'd only seen Mark's plane from a distance. It looked a lot smaller inside than it did on the outside, which surprised her. She was also surprised by the sudden sense of anticipation that swept over her. Flying had always been a luxury she couldn't afford.

Three hours in the air versus two days on a ferry. How was that even possible?

Mark stood beside her as she continued to study her surroundings. Besides the pilot and copilot seats, there were four additional seats. A grey curtain walled off whatever lay behind them. 'What's back there?'

'I had a couple of seats taken out, as I'll be taking on most of Blake's medevacing duties. I still need to outfit the rest of it, but I've been…waiting to find out exactly what I'll need.'

She nodded, wandering back and pulling aside the curtain, only to find the space devoid of anything but a lone stretcher on wheels that was clamped down along the far wall. No other medical equipment, at least none that she could see. 'Where're your supplies?'

'Blake's been planning on helping with that but, seeing as he just got married, I figured he had other things on his mind right now.' Red crept up his neck. 'I mean—'

'I know what you mean.' She tried not to let those gears switch in her head, but the heat traveling through her own system said she wasn't entirely successful.

'I, er, figured we could grab whatever was needed from the clinic if we had a medevac before I'm completely set up.'

Things were normally so chaotic during those times that trying to do anything other than care for the patient and get off the ground as fast as possible was neither wise nor an efficient use of time. 'I could help you pull some stuff together, if you want.'

His brows drew together, so she hurried to add, 'If you've ever done a medevac before you know it's better to have everything in place long before you need it.'

What was she thinking? She obviously wasn't. But she also

didn't want to have to scramble during an emergency if Mark's plane ended up being called into service.

'I guess you're right.' His eyes traveled over the empty space. 'If you could get me a list…'

She hesitated. 'Will filling this area with medical supplies put a crimp in your regular job?'

'I don't normally haul more than four people at a time, and I'm cutting back to a couple of times a week, so the seats I've left up front should be plenty. I'm also going to try to stick to day trips, so I'll be on hand if something comes up at night.'

'I see. As far as a list, I'll need to order some things from Anchorage.' They moved back towards the front, and Sammi stopped in mid-thought. This was the perfect opportunity to make sure she knew exactly where every piece of equipment was. No digging around for IVs or other items. She could set up the back of Mark's airplane like one of the exam rooms at the clinic with certain crucial instruments paired together for ease of use. 'If you have a free weekend coming up, we could make up an inventory and put everything in place.'

Toby's head popped up from his game. 'Can I help?'

Sammi glanced at Mark to see how he'd react to having her son hanging around.

Just as expected, he stiffened for a second then relaxed. 'I don't see why not. In fact, that's a great idea.'

A great idea?

A sudden sense of relief seemed to color his voice. Almost as if he'd rather have Toby there than…

An ache went through her chest. *The man didn't want to be alone with her.*

Why? Did he think she'd try to take a quick trip down memory lane by pinning him to one of the passenger seats and having her way with him?

If so, he could dream on.

She wasn't about to revisit old times, because all they'd brought her had been heartache.

And if Mark could use a child as a shield, so could she.

'Good, it's settled, then,' she said. 'Toby and I will both be at the hangar first thing Saturday morning.'

Something white drifted past the window, just as Sammi made her pronouncement. If they were going to get out of here, now would be a good time. He glanced at her tilted chin, catching a familiar glint of defiance in her eyes.

The sight made him smile, despite the lingering effects of the nightmare he'd had last night. 'In that case, let's get this show on the road.'

He put a hand on the arm of Toby's seat and waited until the boy looked up at him. 'I need you to stay buckled in during the flight, okay? Do you need to use the restroom before we go?'

Toby seemed to consider his question. 'How long is the trip?'

'You've never flown from the mainland before?'

'I don't think so.' He looked to his mother for confirmation. She shook her head.

For some reason, that made Mark's mood plummet even further, as if he'd once again let down a mother and her son. Ridiculous. He'd never promised to take care of them. 'It takes around three and a half hours.'

The child nodded. 'Then I'd probably better try to go.'

'The bathroom's in the very back, through those curtains.'

Toby removed his earbuds and carefully zipped his game system back into his knapsack. It seemed a very adult thing to do. Most kids he knew would have just tossed the thing onto the seat.

When Toby was out of sight, Mark turned to Sammi. 'Do you not like to fly or something?'

'Flying's fine.' She stared at the curtain between her and her son. 'We just can't afford to hop on a plane every time we want to head to the mainland.'

'But you're a doctor.'

'I'm a community health aide,' she corrected. 'I fly when there's a patient who needs to be transported, not for personal convenience. Besides, with what I make…well, the clinic operates on a shoestring budget. It's why Molly had to go back to Anchorage until she can talk the hospital into funding her for another year.'

If anything, that made him feel worse. 'You could let me know when you need to go and I'll take you. It won't cost you anything.'

Why the hell had he just done that?

Her chin lifted, as it had done several times this morning. 'I prefer to pay my own way, thank you.'

'Even if it means risking your son's health?' The words came out harsher than he'd meant them to, and he immediately wanted to swallow them back. Especially when Sammi looked stricken, her teeth digging into the softness of her lower lip. 'Ah, hell, Sam, I didn't mean that the way it sounded.'

She didn't reply, but wrapped her arms around her midsection and turned away. Mark could swear he saw a sheen of moisture in her eyes as she did so. Desperate to undo the damage he'd caused, he moved behind her and laid his hands on her shoulders. Giving them a gentle squeeze, he leaned down to keep his words quiet. 'I know you love that boy…that you'd do anything for him. Let me help. If you feel you have to pay me something, you can take it out in trade.'

'Why bother?' The whispered words made his heart contract.

'Because I can.' He hesitated. 'Because I want to.'

He did. And Mark knew he was treading on dangerous ground here. His dream last night should have warned him, if nothing else. But was this really about his personal comfort? What about doing the right thing?

And offering to fly her was the right thing. He was certain of it.

And maybe by doing so, he could set a few things right between them. Make up for the heartache he'd caused. Even if it couldn't lead anywhere, he might be able to ease Sammi's burden just a bit. If she'd let him. But even as he decided to try, he wondered at the stupidity of such a move. Even now, her warm, feminine scent was drifting over him, bringing back memories that were better off locked away in some deep corner of his mind. But he'd have to find a way to deal with it. This wasn't about him, it was about helping a fellow human being. Someone he'd once cared about deeply.

Deeply enough to leave her behind.

He rested his chin on top of her head, knowing he'd likely never get another chance, and kept his voice low, hoping to coax her into agreeing. 'I'll tell you what, Sam. You help me trick out the plane like a flying ambulance, and...'

Say it!

'And I'll take you back and forth to the mainland as many times as you want.'

CHAPTER SIX

THE murmured words slid past her ear, sending a shiver over her.

Agreeing to his suggestion would be like committing emotional suicide. But the steady pressure of Mark's hands on her shoulders, the warmth of his body filling the gap between them muddled her thoughts. The squeaked 'Okay' was out of her mouth before she could stop it.

All she had to do was take one step back and she'd be in his arms.

She took a shaky breath instead.

As if he'd guessed her thoughts, he lifted his head and gently turned her to face him. His thumb brushed across a track of moisture on her cheek she hadn't realized was there. 'I'm sorry. For what I said a few minutes ago.'

She lifted a shoulder, not trusting her voice.

'It can't be easy,' he murmured, 'raising him alone. Keeping him safe.'

All her insecurities washed over her in an instant. Plenty of women raised children by themselves, and they seemed to have it so together. But there were days when the loneliness of shouldering the burden closed in around her, stealing her breath as surely as her son's asthma stole his.

His eyes searched hers, seeming to read her every thought.

God, he must think she was the most pitiful creature he'd ever come across. 'We manage.'

Her voice cracked, much to her horror. She tried to clear her throat, but that sounded strangled as well.

'Sam.' The thumb that had brushed across her cheek moved sideways as his fingers slid beneath the braid at her nape, his palm so very warm against her skin. His gaze dropped to her mouth.

He was going to kiss her.

The realization swept through her, just as the curtain behind her swished open, and Toby came trotting into the space, his 'All done!' cracking through the air like a whip.

Sammi yanked free so fast that she stumbled backwards, Mark grabbing her arms to keep her from falling into the seat behind her.

She pulled away again without looking at him and gripped the back of Toby's seat, her hands shaking. 'Go ahead and get buckled in, then.'

Through the tiny window, the snow seemed to be falling a little harder, and her nerves, already on edge, took a turn for the worse. She glanced toward Mark, but avoided looking directly at him. 'Are we going to be able to take off in this?'

'It shouldn't be a problem. But we're also leaving a little later than I'd hoped.'

Because he'd been about to kiss her? Because she would have welcomed it, like a fool?

She made sure Toby was secured and then sat in the copilot seat without a word, fastening her own seat belt.

Mark went through the pre-flight checks like the pro he was, inspecting gauges and switches and communicating with the flight tower.

Was she smart to have taken him up on his offer? A single trip was one thing. An open-ended arrangement was something else entirely.

It felt like charity.

Only he did need to get the plane ready for patients. Maybe he didn't want to be beholden to her either. By agreeing to a fair exchange of services, neither party would owe the other a thing.

Yes. That's how she'd look at it. A business deal that had nothing to do with their personal history or whatever feelings she may or may not have once harbored. Those emotions would stay where they belonged.

In the past.

If she was smart, she'd clearly set the tone for how they were going to handle this little exchange. By keeping things businesslike and impersonal, she'd send him a message that said *hands off*. No more freebies or anything else were heading his way.

The adult playboy Mark might be able to get any woman he laid his eyes on, but she wasn't going to be one of them. Not this time. The touching, the whispered words had almost broken through her barriers and taken her to a place where things would not end well.

As he revved up the engines and taxied toward the runway, she kept her mind fixed on that. Letting things get personal—again—would only end in heartache for both of them. If she couldn't do it for herself, she had to do it for the one person who mattered more than anything in this world.

Her son.

Within minutes, they were in the air. Sammi forced her eyes closed, letting the sound of the engines wash over her.

Go to sleep. It's the best thing you can do. For everyone involved.

Besides, if she was asleep, she wouldn't have to talk. And if she didn't have to talk, she could get off this plane without doing or saying anything else stupid. She needed time alone to sort through things and come up with a plan of attack.

That was it. She'd go on the offensive, rather than sit back and worry about how she was going to react to seeing him and Toby working together.

She didn't expect to really sleep, so when Mark's voice came through the headset, telling her they'd be landing in about ten minutes, she jerked upright in her seat, blinking.

Oh Lord, if she'd known she was actually going to fall asleep, she'd have taken the stupid thing off. Better that than have him hear what her ex claimed she did at night. He'd had to shake her awake on more than one occasion. She could only imagine how mortified she'd be if that sound was magnified and piped directly into Mark's ear.

A wave of heat washed over her. She glanced over at him to find him staring at her with raised brows.

Uh-oh.

'Um…I didn't…'

'Snore?'

She put a hand to her forehead. *Heavens.* 'Sorry about that. Couldn't you turn the sound off or something? I'm sure it's not something you'd choose to listen to for three hours straight.'

He smiled, turning on every part of her that she'd just finished switching off.

'I've always kind of liked it, remember?' he said, reminding her that he had indeed heard it on more than one occasion. 'You sound like a kitten purring.'

That's certainly not how Brad had described it. No wonder women fell at Mark's feet in droves. He had those pretty little lines down pat.

'I've heard I sound more like chainsaw, but thanks, anyway.'

'Someone actually said that to you?'

'Oh, yeah. I've heard it from more than one person.' Toby had also teased her about her snoring. Relentlessly. She'd retaliated by buying him a package of multicolored earplugs for Christmas.

Mark's smile disappeared and a muscle tightened in his jaw. 'I see.'

Huh? What was with the stiff answer? He'd been cracking jokes a minute ago.

Only when he avoided her eyes and turned to face forward did she realize how he'd taken her words. That she'd heard about her snoring from more than one *man*.

A spike of anger charged through her gut. What if she had? It was none of his business who she'd slept with. He'd made no secret of hopping from the bed of one beautiful woman to another. Did he think she wasn't attractive enough to land anyone other than him—although look where that had gotten her—and her ex-husband? She could sleep with a million men and it would still have nothing to do with him.

If he'd been a normal person, she might have corrected his misconception. As it was, she didn't feel she owed him any explanation whatsoever.

Fine. Hopefully they'd be on the ground in short order and she could get away from him as fast as humanly possible. Twisting around in her seat, she saw that Toby was still playing his game. He hadn't overheard their conversation, which was a good thing.

Even without his earbuds, the rumble of the twin propellers filled the space, creating a constant drone that was louder than her supposed snoring could ever be.

She hoped Mark liked the sound of those engines, because that's all he'd be hearing from now until they were on the ground.

She needn't have worried, because he didn't try to fill up the time with chatter anyway. He maintained his rigid silence until they whipped down the tiny runway at Dutch Harbor.

As soon as they slowed to a crawl, coasting toward the nearest hangar, Sammi unlatched her seat belt and started to scoot out of her chair. 'Thanks for the lift. I appreciate it.'

'Mind staying in your seat for another minute or two?'

'Why? I don't think it's really—'

The plane came to a sudden halt, and the momentum that should have been absorbed by her seat belt threw her body forward into the instrument panel a few feet away. Her elbow landed with a thud against the nearest metal object. 'Ouch!'

She dropped back into her seat, rubbing her injured limb.

'That's why.' He didn't look the slightest bit sorry that he'd just about killed her.

'You did that on purpose!' she fumed.

'I did ask you to stay seated.'

'Mom, are you okay?' Toby was looking at her with his brows puckered. 'You're not supposed to stand up until the seat belt sign goes off.'

Except there was no sign. Just a smart-ass who evidently had a Napoleon complex. Except this particular Napoleon could never be considered short.

Short-tempered, maybe. She remembered the black eyes he'd sported on more than one occasion from fights he'd been in during their middle- and high-school years. He'd thought he was hiding the truth from her...from everybody, but she'd seen right through the act. Knew his father was responsible for some of those bruises.

'I'm okay. And you're right.' She sent a glare Mark's way. 'You should never stand up while a plane is in motion. *Someone* might get hurt.'

Mark gave a quick sigh as he shut down the engines. 'If I say I'm sorry, can we call a truce?'

'Depends what you're sorry for.'

'Making you fall?'

Would that be making her fall right now? Or making her fall for him years ago?

She'd go with the former option. It was the only smart one. Because the other was unthinkable.

Because no matter what else she did in this lifetime, she wasn't going to fall for Mark Branson ever again.

CHAPTER SEVEN

SAMMI smiled as yet another clucking sound came from the woman beside her. Apparently Hannah, resident physician's assistant and all-round worrywart, had found another problem.

'Okay, spill it.'

Hannah tapped the sheet of paper on the counter between them. 'I see three bags of saline on this list, but no warmer.'

'A warmer. You're right, I didn't even think about it. I'm used to keeping a unit of saline in the glove compartment while en route to a patient, but I guess planes don't have glove compartments, do they?' Sammi slid the paper closer and jotted down a note to check the prices on fluid warmers.

Hannah wrinkled her nose. 'You're kidding right? You don't actually do that.'

'In Unalaska? Where hypothermia is a constant threat? Um…yeah. Pumping cold saline into an already chilled patient isn't going to do him any good. My glove compartment must be near a heater vent because it gets nice and toasty in there. I've heard of throwing them on the dashboard as well.'

The PA's mouth opened and closed a time or two, before anything came out. 'Okay, I guess I'm a little too sheltered. I wasn't saying you should administer cold fluids. Been there, had one of those, and it's not a pleasant experience. I'm saying that's what *war-mers* are for.'

'Warmers cost *mon-ey*.' Sammi mimicked her friend's inflection. 'Maybe I could use that baby wipe warmer I got as a gift when Toby was born.'

'A baby wipe warmer. Really?'

Sammi laughed. Okay, so maybe Hannah was right. But when funds were tight, you found ways to make do. Hannah wasn't from the Aleutians or even Alaska, she'd grown up in Idaho and had moved to the island a little over three months ago, taking the place of the PA who'd retired last year. The lanky redhead had arrived just in time, too, as Molly was no longer around. But the young woman still had a thing or two to learn about medicine in the Aleutians.

'I'm going to bring it in and check it for size. You never know, it might just fit. If not, maybe I can kind of squeeze it inside...'

Hannah rolled her eyes and giggled. 'Squeeze it inside? What if it breaks in the process? I don't think you want to be electrocuted. Just bite the bullet and ask someone for the real thing.'

They'd been so intent on their list that Sammi hadn't heard the door open, but she definitely heard the low drawl that came from somewhere behind her. 'I would ask what it is that might break if it's the wrong size but, quite frankly, I'm afraid to.'

A rush of heat washed through her face as she whirled around and found Mark leaning against the wall beside the entrance. His lazy smile said what his words hadn't quite spelled out: that finding two women giggling over something's size couldn't be good.

She licked her lips, trying to get herself under control, but a nervous laugh came out before she could stop it. 'We weren't talking about... I mean we were trying to figure out how to...'

Hannah came to her rescue. 'We're trying to decide whether to buy an IV warmer for your plane.'

'As opposed to a...' He paused and waited for someone to fill in the blank.

'A—a baby wipe warmer.'

The look on Mark's face was priceless. His eyes widened, his mouth moving as if to repeat the words. Then he laughed. Sounding nothing like Sammi's pitiful snicker of humiliation, Mark's chuckle filled the room with light and mirth, bringing back memories of a younger, less cynical Mark. The joyous sound sent a shiver down her spine.

She stared at him for a few seconds, glancing over at Hannah to find her with her hands plastered over her mouth, shaking with silent laughter of her own.

Okay, it wasn't that funny.

Then why were her lips curving higher as Mark's laughter made its way past a cold, isolated area in her heart, warming it instantly?

She stood a little taller, needing to get control of this situation *and* her silly emotions. 'We'll see who has the last laugh when I bring that baby wipe warmer in tomorrow.'

'This I've got to see.' Mark was still smiling, as if her idea was the most ridiculous thing he'd ever heard.

'Prepare to hear "I told you so." Both of you.'

Hannah choked out, 'You could always put it in the restroom if that doesn't work out. No one likes a cold roll of t-toilet paper.'

'Very funny.' Sammi shook her finger at the two of them. 'Did you both graduate from the same school of future comedians? If so, I don't think you should quit your day jobs.'

Hannah took a deep breath in and let it back out, then crossed to Mark and held out her hand. 'Hannah Lassiter, Unalaska's resident spendthrift, if you believe what Sammi says. Seriously, I'm the new PA.'

Taking her hand and giving it a quick shake, Mark introduced himself as well. Surprisingly enough, he didn't immediately lay on the charm that seemed to have most women clinging to his arm by the end of the encounter. Instead, he was businesslike and professional.

It made her nervous.

What was he up to? She'd never known him to pass up an opportunity like this. He'd even put the moves on Molly when she'd first arrived on the island.

'Did you want something?' she asked, the waspish edge back in her voice.

'I came to make sure we were still on for Saturday. I have to run a tourist to Akutan and won't be back until tomorrow afternoon. Didn't want you to worry.'

Why on earth did he think she would?

She'd been frantic when he'd left that first time. Had hoped and prayed he'd change his mind and come back. Well, he hadn't, and she'd learned her lesson. If he disappeared tomorrow, never to return, she'd barely raise an eyebrow. 'Don't worry. I won't.'

He ignored her churlish words. 'Do you need anything from the island?'

A more civilized tongue, maybe? Except if she suggested it, he might get the idea she was ready to let bygones be bygones. She hadn't quite made it to that point yet, despite the whole turn-the-other-cheek lessons she'd learned in Sunday school years ago.

Besides, she was fresh out of cheeks.

'I can't think of anything.' She glanced at Hannah. 'How about you?'

'Do they have a coffee chain outlet?'

Sammi thought for a second she might be serious, but the other woman's smile gave her away. 'Nope, just the same kind of sludge we have here.' She had a thought. 'Hey, are you heading to Anchorage afterwards?'

'I was planning to. Why?'

She gave Hannah a mock glare. 'Ask Molly if the hospital has any spare IV warmers lying around.'

'You got it. Anything else?'

As she looked at his warm green eyes and solid, steady presence, she found she did want something else despite her best efforts. She wanted a time machine. One that would take her back to simpler days and a very different Mark.

She bit her lip. But then she wouldn't have her son, and he meant everything to her.

She couldn't go back, and neither could Mark. But maybe they could turn a page on their past and start afresh, bypassing the blips and complications that came with a more intimate relationship.

Maybe they could learn to be colleagues. And if they were very lucky, someday they might even become…friends.

He was losing his touch. And maybe even his nerve.

Pulling into his mother's driveway, he made no move to get out of the car. There was a new woman on the island, and he hadn't given her a second glance. The PA was beautiful enough, with reddish mahogany locks that curled loose and free around high classical cheekbones and a delicate upturned nose. He'd willed himself to smile at her, but the knowledge that Sammi was standing right there, probably waiting for him to do just that, kept him from acting.

Or maybe it was the pang of regret that had come from listening to Sammi's laughter as she'd joked with the other woman.

Until she'd seen him standing there.

Then the light in her eyes had flickered out, her chin going up in a defensive move she probably wasn't even aware of. As if waiting for him to hurt her. Again.

It brought back memories of his father and the way the bastard had disappointed his mother repeatedly. And that wasn't the worst of it. Even the thought made his hands ball into fists at his side, something he'd seen his old man do time and time again—just before he'd let loose and used them on whoever was the closest. Mark forced his own fingers to flex and relax.

The second his father had found that engagement ring, Mark had known he had to leave the island, that he couldn't allow

Sammi to be drawn into his nightmare. But in doing so, he'd felt tremendous guilt at leaving his mother alone.

No, that wasn't entirely true. From the time he'd turned eighteen, Mark had pleaded with his mother to leave...to report his father to the authorities, but she'd always refused. Had made up excuses until the day he'd died.

And in running away from one terrible situation, Mark had found himself in the middle of a nightmare of a different sort. One he still struggled with.

He finally went to the door of his childhood home and knocked, before peeking inside. 'Mom? You home?'

'I'm in the kitchen,' she called out.

Walking into the other room, he found her slicing apples over a low table and tipping them into a bowl of water. Fresh lemon slices floated on the surface. He leaned down to kiss her cheek. 'What are you doing?'

'Making an apple pie.' She smiled up at him. 'Your favorite.'

'It is indeed.' He pulled a chair from the small kitchen table that sat in the corner of the room and parked it next to her wheelchair. 'Do you want some help?'

Her brows went up. 'Do I usually?'

'No.'

They never talked about his father. In fact, Mark had never once been to his grave, although he knew his mother put flowers on it from time to time.

Sammi had sent them a sympathy card that had almost made him laugh. Because sorrow had been the last thing he'd felt. He'd felt relief that his mother was finally safe, that she could now live her life without being afraid.

For a few brief moments he'd toyed with the idea that he could come home and make things right with Sammi now that the threat was over, that she might somehow forgive him for leaving her in the first place. In fact, he'd kept the ring all these years, just for that reason.

But his first night back, he'd had a nightmare. The second

night had brought another one. Then he'd seen Toby, and the whole scene at his chopper had played through his mind in agonizing slow motion. How would Sammi feel if she discovered what her son did to his own insides? That when the child's blanket fell away in his dreams, it was sometimes Toby's face he saw and not the dying boy's.

He hated it, despised his mind for playing those kinds of tricks on him, but he was powerless to stop it.

The best he'd been able to accomplish was to hold himself at bay with a string of meaningless relationships—hoping Sammi would take the hint that they were over and done.

Of course, working with her on the plane shot those plans to hell.

He swallowed, forcing back his thoughts by ducking his hand into the icy lemon-water and plucking a slice of apple. The tartness hit his tongue with an acidic rush, forcing his lips to draw up in protest. 'Sour.'

His mom laughed. 'I haven't added the sugar yet. The lemons keep the slices from turning dark and ruining the pie.'

Kind of like the happy-go-lucky attitude Mark had adopted after leaving the military. It kept his mind from wandering into dark places. Or ruining lives. After all, no one wanted to wake up next to a man who cowered beneath the covers whenever he heard a branch crack under the weight of ice, or one who zoned out and saw the death of a child time and time again.

'I came by to let you know I have to work this weekend. I promised Sammi I'd get the plane ready for service.'

'Sammi?' Her knife stopped in mid-slice.

There was such hope in that single word that Mark had to grit his teeth to keep from immediately setting her straight. He knew his mom wanted him to get married someday and provide her with grandchildren, but it wasn't on the cards right now. Maybe it would never be.

He forced a smile and dipped into the water for another slice, taking a bite of the crisp, sour fruit. He studied the flesh before popping the rest into his mouth. His mom was right. The lemon kept the apples as white as snow.

If he could do the same thing, keep his true feelings submerged, he might just get through his time with Sammi unscathed.

But more importantly, so would she.

CHAPTER EIGHT

'HEY, Mom, can I try out the bed?' Toby pushed his hand against the thin mattress of the stretcher.

They'd come to the airport loaded with supplies and equipment. Hannah had insisted on showing up at the clinic and helping her pile everything into her tiny car. Sammi had been tempted to ask the other woman to come to the airport with them, but couldn't bring herself to. Hannah's week had been hectic, and she deserved some downtime. So Sammi and Toby went to face Mark together. At least she had her son along with her for the ride.

She started to tell Toby not to climb on the stretcher, but Mark came over with another box of bandages, catching the tail end of his question. 'Sure, bud, go ahead. It's not very comfortable, though.'

How on earth did Mark know that? Yeah, well, some thoughts were better left unexplored.

Her son scrambled onto the mattress and sat there, legs dangling over the side. 'If I get hurt really bad, is this where I'll have to stay? I couldn't ride in the seat like I did last time, right?'

Sammi's heart crawled into her throat and lodged there. She'd had nightmares of him having an attack serious enough to require a medevac. It was one thing to be a half-hour from a hospital like he'd been during his episode at the zoo. It was another thing entirely to get onto a plane knowing it would take three and a half hours to reach a medical facility. So many things could happen in that time.

When she glanced at Mark, she noted his face was devoid of any color and his hands gripped the back of a seat with such force that his knuckles stood out. Before she could ask him what was wrong, he seemed to recover, pulling in a deep breath. 'Yes. This is where you'd be. But you don't have to worry about that. We're going to try to make sure you stay good and healthy.'

We? The lump in her throat grew.

'I have asthma, you know.'

'I know.' Mark didn't try to minimize her son's announcement, he simply acknowledged it.

That satisfied Toby, and he quickly switched to another subject. 'My mom is going to help with the patients, isn't she?'

'Sometimes.'

Mark seemed completely at ease again. The relaxed façade he showed to the world was back in place. But she'd just glimpsed something she might have missed had she not been watching.

Her son glanced up at her. 'Will I stay with Grandma when you're helping sick people?'

'Yes.' Sammi's mother already knew this was a possibility, and she was more than thrilled to keep Toby. It made Sammi nervous to leave him alone overnight, but she'd done it before Molly had come to the island. The problem was she'd gotten used to going home every night, safe in the knowledge she wouldn't have to make any sudden runs to Anchorage. Yep, she was definitely spoiled.

Her eyes fastened on a shoebox-sized box Mark was cutting open with a knife. She caught the words *"Fluid War—"* before the top opened and revealed what looked like a rectangular insulated bag.

She couldn't remember ordering anything that looked like... 'What's that?'

Glancing down, then back up, his eyes met hers. 'My contribution to the supplies.'

'An IV warmer? Is that from Alaska Regional?'

'No. I know funds are tight, so—'

'You bought one? I told you I'd try my baby wipe warmer. Toby's growing up, so I don't need it any more.'

'You never know.' Something flashed behind Mark's eyes before he extinguished it. 'You might have another child someday.'

Right. It wasn't as if she had men lined up, waiting to take her out. And after her failed marriage, she couldn't see herself jumping into another relationship.

She wasn't like Mark. Or her father who—like Mark—oozed charm and had used it every chance he'd got...to the chagrin of his wife. Sammi couldn't bounce from relationship to relationship. She needed a strong connection before getting involved. Something in common. Because of that, she'd always thought she'd be married for life.

How quickly things could change.

Staring at the zippered warmer, an ache went through her chest. She wanted someone who really heard her. Someone who went the extra mile to make sure she knew she was loved.

That someone wasn't Mark, despite the fact that his purchase made her gushy inside, made her want to wrap her arms around him with a sigh and absorb some of his warmth and strength.

In fact, it might just be one of the nicest things anyone had ever done for her.

That damned moisture was gathering in the back of her eyes again.

Mark must have sensed something was wrong, because he added, 'I know the clinic doesn't have the funds to buy one, but Hannah made it sound pretty important.'

'She's right. It is.' She hesitated, trying to figure out a way to thank him that wouldn't come across as pathetic and needy. Or make the stinging in her eyes even worse. 'Thank you. I'm sure the patients will appreciate it.'

'I'm sure they will.' A beat went by. 'But what about you, Sam? Did I do the right thing?'

Something about the way he said it—the almost pleading note that hovered between them—caused little sparks to go off in her stomach, spreading outward and setting off more explosive charges along the way.

Act like you don't care one way or the other.

But she did care. And lying wouldn't do anyone any good. He'd made an effort. The least she could do was acknowledge it.

'You did.' The words came out as a whisper.

Mark straightened, standing far too close for her emotional well-being, the warmer still gripped in his hand.

Her lips parted as he brushed back a strand of hair that had drifted across her cheek.

'What the heck's an IV warmer?' Just like that, Toby shattered the moment by jumping off the stretcher.

As jarring as it was, Sammi could have kissed him for yanking her back to her senses. She sidestepped Mark and did just that. 'It keeps bags of medicine warm so the patients don't get cold when we give it to them.'

'Oh.'

When she glanced at Mark, she saw he was staring at his hand, a far-away look in his eyes. The shadow of a bruise was still visible from where she'd slammed the door on it.

Was he thinking about her?

Of course not.

A thread of anger twisted inside her. This was getting ridiculous. She wasn't an eighteen-year-old girl any more. She couldn't turn starry-eyed every time Mark said or did something nice. He'd do the same for any woman. He'd proved that time and time again.

She was no one special.

He'd driven that home in the cruelest possible way. And she needed to be on her guard from here on out. That mark on his hand pulled at her conscience, though, as did the memory of those old breaks.

'How's your hand, by the way?'

He blinked, his face hardening slightly. 'My hand?'

'Where the door caught it.' She touched the bruise, the yellow color signifying it was healing. 'Any lingering problems?'

He stuffed the IV warmer into an overhead bin, effectively pulling away from her touch. 'None. I'd almost forgotten about it.'

A pang went through her. Maybe she'd better just leave him to do the rest of the set-up on his own. 'Well, I guess we're about done here—'

The buzzer sounded on her phone, stopping her from making a quick getaway. She glanced at the readout. Hannah.

Clicking the talk button, she put the phone to her ear. The receiver crackled with static. 'Hey, Hannah. What's up?'

'I...' The voice faded, the one word sounding shaky and uncertain.

'Hannah? Is everything okay?'

'Not sure...' The PA seemed to be struggling with her thoughts.

'Do you have a patient?'

'Y-yes.'

Sammi waited, but only heard the sound of heavy breathing. 'Hannah? Who's the patient?'

'I...' a groan came across the line. 'I think...I think it's me.'

Mark's glance traveled beyond the flashing lights of the police car and found the wreck itself. The front of the car was crumpled, and two officers were working on the driver's-side door, trying to force it open. Sammi gasped from the seat beside him. 'Oh, God. Hannah.'

She leaped from the vehicle almost before they'd pulled to a complete stop, her medical bag gripped in her right hand.

'Mom!' Toby's frightened voice came from the back seat. 'What's happening?'

Putting the car in park and feeling more impotent than he ever had in his life, Mark twisted in his seat to face Toby, the child's pale, scared features pulling at him in the worst possible way. 'Your mom went to help Hannah. It's okay.'

The back of the plane wasn't even completely set up yet. If they had to medevac her out…

Could Sammi do it?

Yes, she'd proved herself to be competent and inventive. She'd be able to handle just about anything.

Unlike him. Maybe he shouldn't have agreed to take on this gig. His military flight training should have prepared him for any eventuality. He'd had to ferry injured soldiers back from distant battlegrounds. Had had to watch helpless as a young child died inside his chopper, as that child's mother, swathed with explosive charges, had run away from the plane at the last minute, trying to spare Mark and her son.

He swallowed the sour taste that rose in the back of his throat.

Those memories had the power to make him lose track of where he was…of who he was with.

But he wasn't in his chopper now. He was here in Dutch Harbor with a little boy who needed him to keep it together.

'Toby.' He faced the child again. 'This is important. Do you know your grandmother's phone number?'

'Of course. I'm not three.' Color poured back into the child's face.

'I'm going to ask her to come pick you up.' He handed over his cell phone. 'Can you punch in the number?'

Toby nodded, taking the phone from him and jabbing the buttons in rapid succession. 'There.' He gave the phone back.

Three rings…four…

Come on, pick up.

The screech of metal giving way met his ears and he saw the door pull free of the car. Sammi was next to it in an instant.

'Hello?'

'Mrs. Trenton? This is Mark Branson, remember me?'

There was a slight pause then her voice came over the line, the chill in it unmistakable. 'Yes, of course I do.'

He ignored the pointed words, knowing he deserved whatever censure she tossed at him, but it would have to wait until later. 'Can you come and pick up Toby? There's been an accident—'

'Sammi?' The coolness in her tone gave way to fear.

'No, no, she's fine. We're at an accident scene and may have to do a medevac. I think she said you were to watch Toby if that happened.'

'I'll be right there. Tell me where you are.'

Mark quickly relayed their location and clicked off when Sammi's mom said she'd be there in less than ten minutes.

'Get your stuff together, buddy.'

'I don't have any.'

Mark frowned. 'What about your inhaler?'

The child's eyes widened. 'I think I left it on the plane.' Then Toby breathed out a sigh. 'But Grandma always has an extra one at her house.'

'Good.' Mark made a mental note to ask, then focused on keeping Toby's attention away from the ruined vehicle once he noted efforts to extricate Hannah were under way. He sent up a quick prayer, hoping it wasn't as bad as it looked, then said, 'Hey, do you know how to play I Spy?'

The next several minutes were taken up with searching out innocuous items, making sure to choose things in or near the ocean, which faced away from the scene of the accident.

'No, it's not the rock,' Mark said.

A small grey Toyota pulled up behind them, and Mark saw

with relief that it was Sammi's mother. 'Wait here for a second, okay?'

He clicked his door open and waved to the older woman, who hurried toward them.

'Oh, my God, who's in there, do you know?'

'Hannah Lassiter. She works at the clinic with Sammi.'

Grace Trenton shook her head. 'I know Hannah. Poor girl, is she going to be okay?'

'I don't know. I've been letting Sammi and the police do their jobs.'

'Toby?'

'In the car.' He touched Grace's arm. 'Listen, Toby said you had another inhaler. He left his on my plane when we were over there, setting up.'

'I do. I keep a couple of extras on hand.' She glanced again toward the accident. 'Looks like I'll be keeping my grandson for the night.'

'Is that okay?'

'Of course. I'll take him now so she doesn't worry.' She gave Mark a hard look. 'I'm going to say this one time then you won't hear me mention it again. I know you have to work together, and Sammi may look and act tough. She's not. Neither is Toby. For my daughter's sake, please...*please* don't start something you don't intend to finish.'

Before he had a chance to understand what she meant, she'd moved away and had opened the car door to collect Toby. The child leaped out and hugged his grandmother around the waist. Grace took his hand and led him to her car, the boy turning to wave wildly at Mark as he went, a smile plastered to his face.

Mark started to wave back, then Grace's warning went through his head, her meaning finally taking hold and burrowing deep: *Don't start something you don't intend to finish.*

Like he had eight years ago?

If that's what she meant, Mark couldn't agree more. And he intended to keep reminding himself of that advice over and over.

For as long as it took to make himself believe it.

CHAPTER NINE

'HELP me!'

Sammi threw the words at Mark, who stood frozen beside the closed door of the plane, his eyes vacant.

Why wasn't he moving?

They'd made it to the airfield, but she didn't dare let him go to the cockpit until they'd stabilized Hannah's breathing, which had grown increasingly labored as they'd rushed to the airport. The steering-wheel that had pinned the still unconscious PA to her seat had almost certainly sent a rib through the woman's left lung, as Sammi wasn't getting many breath sounds when she listened on that side. Hannah's blood pressure was also dropping. And Mark hadn't moved in the last two or three minutes.

'Hey!' she yelled again. 'Come on. I need you over here, dammit. Now!'

He appeared to shake himself back to the present and crossed over to her. 'Sorry. What do you want me to do?'

Ripping open Hannah's white blouse, and praying she was right, she splashed some Betadine high on Hannah's chest, making sure it hit the area where the second intercostal space was located.

'I have to decompress her chest, so she can breathe better. There should be a box of needles in one of the drawers. I know we haven't separated them yet, but I need you to dig through the container and find one that says fourteen gauge. If you can't find it, just get me the biggest needle you can find. And the longest.'

Mark, seemingly back to his old self, tore through the supplies, while Sammi scrambled to get an IV set up.

'Sorry, honey,' she murmured to Hannah as she inserted a line. 'I don't have time to get the warmer out.' And with the temperature outside dropping rapidly, the interior of the plane was growing ever colder. So much so that a quick shudder rippled through her as she hung the bag of saline on a nearby hook. She forced it back, knowing she couldn't afford to let the tremors move down to her hands.

Eyes burning, she remembered laughing with Hannah about the dangers of pumping cold fluids into a patient. She'd never dreamed it would be one of them lying on that table.

She straightened up and caught herself. Now was not the time to be emotional. Hannah would do exactly the same thing if she were in her shoes.

'Found one.'

'Open the wrapper and hand it to me.' Sammi had already slapped on a pair of gloves, but didn't have time to tell Mark to do the same. It should be okay, as long as he didn't click off the protective cover.

He put it into her waiting palm, and Sammi twisted the cap, exposing the needle. Using her free hand, she found Hannah's clavicle then moved down to the second rib and the space just beneath it. 'Stand back.'

No time for a mask. No time for second thoughts.

Please let it be air compressing that lung and not blood from an internal bleeder.

Before she had time to change her mind, she pressed the needle home. She felt the quick *pop* as it entered the pleura, followed by a gurgle, then air hissed from the site.

Air!

No symphony ever written was as beautiful as that sound.

The left side of Hannah's chest deflated as the trapped air continued to escape. Within a minute the woman's breathing eased, and Sammi was able to gently retract the needle.

'Hell, Sam. I can't believe you just did that.'

She glanced up to find Mark staring at her, every bit of color drained from his face.

'If I hadn't, she'd have died.'

'I know, it's just...' He swallowed, his Adam's apple dipping before coming back up. 'You've changed.'

'Yeah, well, so have you.' The paralyzed version of Mark she'd seen a few minutes ago had scared her almost as much as Hannah's injuries. And the look on his face as he'd watched her work... A sliver of fear skittered through her. Was there something wrong with him?

No time to think about that right now.

She turned away and checked Hannah's vitals. Her blood pressure had come back up. 'We can take off now.'

'Right.' Without another word, Mark turned away. Out of the corner of her eye she noted the shaky fingers raking through his thick dark hair, the jerky movements as he did what she asked.

What was going on? He was always so cool. So sure of himself.

Something had shaken him. Hannah's condition? No, she didn't think that was it.

Forget about it.

She could try to figure it out later. Right now she needed to concentrate on her friend and pray all three of them could hold it together for the next three hours. Until they reached Anchorage.

She'd had to perform the needle decompression twice more on the trip, and she damned herself for not making sure a catheter had been loaded onto the plane. But there was nothing to do about it now, except make sure Hannah's chest cavity stayed clear of air.

'Better?' she asked.

Hannah had regained consciousness minutes after they were airborne, and while that was an encouraging sign, Sammi cringed each time she had to stick her to relieve the growing pressure.

'Yes.'

'I'm so sorry, Hannah.'

The other woman reached out and touched Sammi's hand, her voice gravelly and weak. 'Don't. It's better than suffocating.'

Sammi gritted her teeth, unable to answer. She busied herself checking her friend's vitals, which were still holding steady. 'How do your ribs feel?'

'Like I've been hit. With a baseball bat,' Hannah managed to get out.

'You were, kind of. The steering-wheel had pinned you to the seat. It's a wonder you were able to call me.'

Hannah shook her head. 'I knew if I didn't try…'

Neither of them needed her to finish that phrase, knowing what probably would have happened if she hadn't.

Glancing at her watch, she patted Hannah on the shoulder. 'Let me see how much longer.'

A storm had been riding their tail almost the whole way, making it a bumpy flight. She moved to the front, where Mark was working the controls with a much steadier hand than he'd had earlier. 'You okay? You were acting kind of strange a while back.'

His jaw tightened. 'Fine. How's the patient?'

'No signs of internal bleeding or head trauma. Do we have an ETA?'

He glanced up at her. No sign of the haunted look he'd worn as she'd worked on Hannah. 'Around ten minutes.'

'Good. I'm hoping the broken rib and punctured lung are as bad as things get. No way to know the full extent of the damage until they get some chest CTs.'

'CTs?'

'Cat scans. Sorry. I keep forgetting you're not an EMT.'

'That's probably a good thing.'

She smiled. 'At least you didn't faint. Although you had me worried for a few minutes there.'

Her second attempt to get him to open up was met with as much enthusiasm as her first. Something flickered behind his eyes for a second then he turned his attention back to the sky in front of him.

'You're good,' he said. 'If I were injured, I'd want you working on me.'

A quick jab of shock went through her. If she hadn't seen his face, she'd think he was joking, but the tight lines around his eyes said he was dead serious. She had no idea why he'd felt the need to say something like that, but the thought of him lying on that stretcher—hurting—did ugly things to her composure. 'Let's hope it never comes to that.'

He nodded. 'I'll let you get back to it.'

Sammi studied his stiff profile for a second longer before heading back to Hannah's side. Her patient's eyes were closed, and she frowned.

'Hannah?'

The other woman groaned. 'Can't a body get some sleep?'

'No.' The tension drained from her lungs. 'Not on my watch. No sleeping until we get you to the hospital.'

Mark called for them to prepare for landing. Already she could sense the floor beneath her feet tilting as they made their descent.

Checking the wheels on the stretcher yet again to be sure they were locked in place, she sat in the seat next to the bed, and held Hannah's hand. 'The landing's probably not going to feel good on those ribs.'

'Nothing feels good right now.' She glanced over her head at the IV bag, which was swaying on its hook. 'I guess I didn't rate the baby wipe warmer.'

Sammi laughed, glad Hannah was feeling well enough to joke. 'No time to test it, remember?'

The wheels touched down with a couple of hard bumps, and Hannah's smile transformed into a grimace as they jostled and bounced their way to a stop.

'You holding on okay?'

Hannah gasped. 'Remind me…to lodge a complaint…with the pilot.'

'I will. Once we get you back on your feet again.'

Thankfully Molly was on duty today and had promised to meet them. One of the legs of the runway ran almost up to the hospital's entrance so they could basically wheel Hannah down the ramp of the plane and through the sliding glass doors.

Mark powered down, then came back to help ready Hannah for transport. Sure enough, as soon as the door to the plane swung open, a small contingent of doctors and nurses came into view, Molly's familiar face among them.

They wheeled Hannah down to ground level, Molly running over to meet them. 'What have we got?'

Everyone was all business. 'Hannah Lassiter, twenty-nine years old, car accident, possible broken rib with accompanying pneumothorax on the left side. I did three needle decompressions, but the chest keeps filling back up. She'll probably need a chest tube and a CT. Vitals are stable, BP one-twenty over eighty, pulse eighty-five. I couldn't measure her pulse ox.'

Molly nodded, leaning over the gurney with her stethoscope. 'Hannah, how are you doing? Any pain?'

'What do you think?' Hannah took a breath, gasping as she did. 'I think I'm going to need that chest tube pretty quickly.'

'We'll get you one.' Molly motioned to a nearby attendant. 'Let's get her inside.'

Turning to Sammi, she smiled. 'You know the routine. We'll take it from here.'

Sammi nodded, leaning down to kiss Hannah's cheek.

'You'd better come home soon.' She glanced at Molly. 'And you had *better* call me as soon as I can see her.'

'Will do.' Molly followed the stretcher into the hospital, already calling out orders for tests and treatments.

A minute or two went by as she and Mark stood just inside the entrance.

'Well, I guess that's that,' she said. 'Feels kind of weird, huh?'

'Hmm.' Hands propped low on his hips, he didn't seem to be in a hurry to talk about anything.

Okay, so this was going to be awkward if every medevac wound up like this. She wrapped her arms around her waist to ward off the chilly air that had followed them inside. 'Do you need to take the plane to the hangar?'

'I guess I do.' He didn't move, though, and Sammi wasn't sure why he was hesitating all of a sudden. Maybe he was trying to figure out a subtle way to head back to the island. Now.

Although Mark didn't normally do subtle.

As if reading her thoughts, he touched her arm. 'Listen, I'm sorry about earlier.'

'Earlier?'

'Before we took off. I was…distracted.'

That wasn't quite the word Sammi would have chosen, but she was at a loss to find a better one.

Horrified? Scared?

No, neither of those fit either.

A nurse walking down the corridor glanced toward them, and then did a double take. 'Mark?'

His hand fell away from Sammi's arm as the woman crossed over to them. Tall and slender, her blonde hair was twisted into an elegant knot. Not a single strand was out of place.

Sammi fingered her own messy braid, wishing she'd had time to do something different with it. She tossed it over her shoulder in an effort to hide it.

Ridiculous. Who cares what you look like? You just saved a friend's life.

The woman stopped in front of them. 'Molly said we'd be seeing a lot more of you around here.' Her voice was low and husky, the smile she sent him matching it to perfection.

Throwing a quick glance Sammi's way before he answered, Mark shifted his weight from the balls of his feet to his heels. 'I don't know about that. It depends on how many patients we have to transport.'

Maybe she should try to make a quick exit. This woman certainly seemed like she knew Mark. Quite well, in fact.

What if he wanted to pick up where he'd left off, but didn't want to do it in front of her? Far be it from her to cramp his style.

She looked at the glass doors behind them, where the plane still sat. 'Do you need to get back to Dutch Harbor? If so, don't let me keep you. I'm going to head to the cafeteria and wait for word on Hannah's condition.'

When she started to move away, Mark's fingers circled her wrist, stopping her in her tracks. 'I was planning on spending the night. I try not to do round trips in a single day, if I can help it. Once the plane's put away, I'll join you.'

A shivery sensation went through her that had nothing to do with the cold. He hadn't tried to get rid of her. In fact, he seemed to be using her as a way to give Gorgeous Nurse What's-Her-Name the royal brush-off.

The other woman evidently took the hint, since her delicately carved brows lifted. 'I'll catch you next time you come in, then.' Her sharp gaze zeroed in on Sammi. 'Good luck.'

The acid tone behind the words said it all: *good luck pinning this one down.*

With that the nurse swung away, her hips twitching as if to let Mark know exactly what he'd turned down. Sammi could imagine far too well. And there was no way she'd be able to compete with a woman like that. Ever.

Even if she wanted to. *Which* she didn't.

She tugged her wrist free. 'Okay, then. I'll see you when you're done.'

'Give me about thirty minutes to hand the plane off.'

Sammi nodded. 'As soon as Molly returns and we have a quick cup of coffee, I'll help you get the plane cleaned up. Probably not a good idea to leave the back the way it is.'

'Right. I hadn't thought about that.' He dragged a hand through his hair, looking like he wanted to say something more, but if he did, the words didn't make it out. 'I'll be back as soon as I can.'

'No hurry.'

Mark gave her one last enigmatic look, then turned and walked through the sliding doors.

She shook off her unease. Ever since Hannah had been injured he'd been acting strangely. Scratch that. He'd been this way ever since he'd returned home from the military.

Well, she wasn't going to figure it out by standing here. Besides, she needed to call her mom and let her know she'd made it, and check on Toby.

She wandered to the emergency-room waiting area and dropped into the nearest chair. Not too busy for this time of day. Dialing the number and reaching her mom on the second ring, she was glad to hear laughter in the background.

'Sounds like everything's going okay there.'

Her mom's voice was slightly breathless. 'We're playing duck, duck, goose.'

'Huh? There are only two of you.'

'No, there's also Woody, a penguin and some kind of shark.'

Sammi laughed. 'I'm sure those guys are getting a lot of the action. Don't let him wear you out.'

'He's not. I'm doing the stuff I should have done when you were little.'

'You did, Mom.' Her chest ached every time her mother

went down this road. 'You were working, and there was a lot of…stuff to deal with.'

'You're a good daughter, Sammi.'

'And you're a good mother.' The two of them had played this same game many times before. Their relationship was good, and Sammi was more grateful for her than ever. 'Does he want to talk to me?'

A second later, Toby came on the line. 'Hi, Mom. Is Hannah okay?'

'She will be. The doctors are taking good care of her.'

'Oh.' There was a pause. 'Are you coming home soon?'

Was that a tinge of disappointment she heard in his voice? 'I think I'll need to stay here tonight. Is that okay?'

'Sure! Oh, I mean…sure.' His voice went from happy to dejected in an instant. Trying not to sound too relieved to have his doting grandmother as a playmate for the evening.

Poor Mom.

She smiled. 'Okay. Put Grandma back on, then. Love you.'

Her mom reassured her that they were fine, that she wouldn't let Toby eat too many sweets or stay up too late. And, yes, she had his inhaler nearby.

Ringing off, Sammi sighed and stared at the wall-mounted television, letting the drone of strangers' voices wash over her for a while, glad to have a little time to recuperate before facing Mark again. She glanced down at her watch. Hannah had been in the back for close to an hour.

Just as she started to get up to hunt someone down to see if there was any news, Molly hurried down the corridor, her normally cheerful smile absent as she spotted her and headed over.

Sammi lurched to her feet, a sliver of worry lodging in her gut. Hannah had seemed stable when they'd brought her in, despite the pneumothorax. Had she taken a turn for the worse?

Once Molly reached her, her friend put a hand on her arm. 'Sorry to take so long, the emergency room had another serious case to deal with. I just finished with it.'

'Is Hannah okay?'

'Yes. She's in surgery to repair the damage to her ribs. It shouldn't be much longer.'

'Thank God.'

'It's a good thing you guys got her here when you did, though. The hole in her lung was bigger than expected. Another hour and she might not have made it.'

The words brought back the memory of Mark pressed flat against the metal skin of the plane, something terrible behind his eyes. If he hadn't snapped out of it, what would have happened? Dozens of different scenarios played through her mind, none of them reassuring, because they all ended with Mark paralyzed while Hannah slipped away into darkness.

'Yes,' she said slowly. 'It's a very good thing.'

CHAPTER TEN

MARK made his way across the tarmac, hunched against the snow. The word in the hangar was that the storm that had trailed them from the Aleutians was definitely headed ashore. That storm, however, could be no worse than the one currently raging within his gut.

Why had he ever thought he could run medevacs without being affected by them? Without remembering what had happened in Afghanistan? He could kill Blake for talking him into it.

Therapeutic, his ass.

As was Blake's assertion that battlefield evacs were very different from the sterile medical evacuations practiced in civilian circles. What a crock. The war that Sammi had fought in the belly of his plane had been anything but sterile.

And he hadn't been able to move a muscle as memories of chest compressions and severed limbs paraded through his skull in rapid succession. And that child he'd flown back to the M.A.S.H. unit—little Ahmed. He could still hear the shouts of the medics as they'd worked on him, willing the boy to fight, to breathe. But the damage had been too great.

His breath hitched, even now. Heaven help him, it was still hard for him to look at Toby without remembering that horrific night.

And what if Toby's asthma took a turn for the worse? He'd already been to the emergency room once.

Mark firmed his chin. He might not have been able save one child, but he could make sure Toby didn't ride on the open deck of a boat to reach the mainland.

He was doubly glad Toby wouldn't be on that boat during the incoming storm.

According to the guys at the hangar, the weather would only get worse as the evening wore on, which meant his comment about spending the night was probably carved in stone at this point. The problem was, the icy conditions were supposed to last through tomorrow as well.

The episode at the plane had left him shaken and tired. Having that run-in with the nurse hadn't helped. It had made him take a hard look at his lifestyle and wonder if his strategy for shaking the horror of the past eight years was even feasible. Maybe he'd never be rid of it, no matter what kind of mind games he played with himself.

It was one thing when Sammi hadn't been around to witness him in action, it was another thing entirely to do it right under her nose. He couldn't even remember the nurse's name. That fact ate at him like a school of piranhas tearing flesh from the bone.

How had he gotten to this point?

Becoming a hermit suddenly looked pretty damn good. One thing was certain. He couldn't go on the way he had. Something had to give.

He made it through the hospital entrance and noted that Sammi was no longer standing where he'd left her. Neither was she in the waiting room. He could only hope she'd gone to the cafeteria like she'd mentioned doing. Turning down the corridor to the right, he made his way there, seeing Sammi's dark braid even before he entered the room. Facing away from him, her shoulders were rolled forward, a white coffee cup sitting in front of her.

He moved in front of the table and waited for her to glance up at him. 'You okay?'

'Yes.'

Her one-word reply put him on edge. She'd seen him flip out on the plane, was probably wondering just what she'd been saddled with. Hell, sometimes he wondered that about himself. Blake had left the military without any lasting effects, while he...

Block it out.

'How's Hannah?'

'She's in surgery, but Molly thinks she'll make it through just fine.'

He pulled out the chair across from hers. 'That's great.'

She sighed and fingered her coffee cup. 'I haven't been on one of these runs in a long time. And to have to work on some-one I'm close to, this first time...'

'I know.' He reached out and took her hand, trying not to let the relief swamp him. There was no hint that she was hung up on what had happened earlier.

'Just a few days ago we were laughing about stuffing a sa-line bag into a baby wipe warmer. And then to see her lying on that stretcher, not sure if she was going to live or die...'

He knew exactly what she meant. He'd seen close buddies wheeled off his plane and wondered if he'd ever see them again.

'She's going to be fine, Sammi.'

She tightened her fingers around his. 'I know.'

He glanced down at their joined hands, trying not to think about how natural the act felt. As if he was coming home. As if this was where he belonged.

Wrong. He belonged on the periphery. Arm's length from ev-eryone who mattered. Tonight had proved that beyond a shadow of a doubt. What if Sammi had been lying on that stretcher and he'd zoned out, unable to move...to help.

He should pull away, but somehow he couldn't force him-self to budge. This was a one-time thing. He was simply letting her know he understood how she felt. More so than she might realize.

'Do you need to call Hannah's family and let them know?'

Her eyes met his. 'I never thought to ask for her contact numbers. Maybe in her file…' Her teeth came down on her lip. 'How could I not know if she has family?'

'She has you, Sam. And I can't think of anyone I'd rather have on my side.'

It was the truth. And if he'd been born in a different time and place, he could have ended up with everything he'd ever dreamed of.

She squeezed his hand and let it go. 'Thank you for saying that.'

'So do you want to wait here?'

'I do. Molly's supposed to let me know when I can see her.' She wrapped her hands around her mug and shivered. 'My coffee's cold.'

He eased her fingers away and picked up the cup. 'I'll get you a fresh one. Still cream and sugar?'

'Yes, the same as I…'

She stopped, but Mark knew what she'd been about to say. *The same as I always take it.*

Out of all the women he'd dated since Sammi, how was it that he remembered exactly how she took her coffee, even after all these years? He couldn't recall the name of the nurse in the hallway but he seemed to remember everything about Sammi.

Because she happened during your formative years. Because her memory—and that ring—were what kept you going for the last eight years.

He stood in a rush to shake off that last thought and went to the coffee pot, refilling Sammi's mug and getting one for himself. By the time he made it back to the table, he'd pulled himself together. Partially, anyway.

Sitting down and sliding the cup over to her, he said, 'Let me know if it's not sweet enough.'

She took a sip, not quite meeting his eyes. 'It's fine, thank you.'

Taking a swig of his own coffee and letting it sear its way down his throat, he hoped the caffeine would kick-start his brain and set it down on safer ground. 'Did they say how long surgery would take? You can't sit here all night.'

'No. But I can't leave without seeing her.' Her eyes finally made contact with his. 'Go ahead to the hotel, Mark. No sense in both of us waiting. I know you need to get some rest for the flight tomorrow.'

Should he tell her about the storm coming in?

No. It was just one more thing for her to worry about. 'Did you get a hold of your mom?'

She nodded. 'She and Toby were in the middle of playing a game.'

'He's stayed with her before.'

'Lots of times.' A tiny smile appeared. 'They're best of friends. Since Toby's father isn't…around, it's been nice that Mom has been willing to watch him.'

'Your mom is a great person,' he said.

'She is.' Sammi's brows went up. 'So is yours. I could never figure out why she didn't leave, though.'

'Leave?'

Her eyes held his, relaying her meaning without the words having to be said.

He sighed. 'I don't know. I wanted her to.'

'You did, though.' She glanced down at her cup. 'Leave, I mean.'

Is that what she thought? That he'd left to save his own skin? That he'd put his comfort above what they'd had together?

And if she did? Maybe it was better to leave it that way. To let her to draw whatever conclusions she wanted.

'It was complicated, Sammi.' He downed the last of his coffee, forcing the bitter liquid past the lump in his throat. 'Do you want another one?'

'No, I'm good.' She stood. 'I think I'll go back to the waiting room and see if there's any news.'

'Hannah's going to be fine.' He hesitated. 'But are you?'

'What do you mean?'

'If she's here for the next week or so recovering, how are you going to handle the workload?'

'I'll manage.'

He frowned. 'You're already working yourself into the ground. What about Toby?'

Her teeth came down on her lip. 'What else can I do? I can't just walk away from my patients when the going gets tough. The people relying on me are not just tourists looking for thrills. They have real problems.'

As soon as the words came out of her mouth she put her hand to her face, eyes wide. 'Oh, Mark, I didn't mean that the way it came out.'

Yes, she did, and although the inference stung, she was right. He'd purposely chosen a career that didn't involve life-or-death races against the clock. Or downing one too many whiskeys when the clock won.

Hell, he'd drunk himself into a stupor after Ahmed's death. Had had to be carried back to his tent.

It was then the nightmares had begun.

He'd done his best to work through them. Had thought he'd finally succeeded in pushing past the worst of it. Until he'd seen Toby, and the downward spiral had begun all over again.

'It's okay.' He picked up both their cups. 'Are you ready?'

'Yes, but, really, you don't have to sta—'

'No buts. For once, I'm not walking away.' Yes, part of that statement was referring to her earlier words, but he was also talking about his decision eight years ago. When he'd walked away from the best thing that had ever happened to him.

She laid her hand on his arm, her fingers finally warm again after their flight. 'I'm sorry for saying that. I don't deal well with uncertainty.'

He smiled and covered her hand with his own. 'Are you kidding? You've always been a rock. Whereas I, on the other hand, was always a royal screw-up.'

Retrieving his coat from the back of the chair, they made their way to the waiting room and sat in chairs next to each other. An uneasy truce seemed to have sprung up between them, one he was loath to mess up. So he stuck to small talk, which he murmured in a low voice to avoid disturbing others who also waited for word on their loved ones. He figured that by droning on and on, Sammi didn't have to think, she could just sit back and not expend any more energy than she already had. So it was a shock when in the middle of a sentence, he felt something land on his shoulder.

He turned his head slightly, and his chin brushed Sammi's forehead.

She was asleep. Exhausted.

No longer needing to talk, he sat there and absorbed each tiny nuance of her. The pressure of her cheek against his shoulder, the slightly medicinal scent of lemon and antiseptic that now clung to her. The heavy breathing that he knew from experience could quickly turn into that cute kittenish snore. Leaning a little closer, he let the wall he'd erected between them lower a couple of inches. Just enough so that he could allow his jaw to rest on the silky hair on top of her head.

'Your wife's tired.'

A whispered voice came from a woman two chairs over.

Shock went through him, and he started to correct her assumption, explaining they were just coworkers. But how many colleagues would drape themselves over each other like this?

Okay, so Sammi falling asleep on him had been an innocent gesture. Not so innocent was his rubbing against her like a cat. So he settled for nodding slightly and scooting down in his chair, hoping that by closing his eyes, he could pretend he too had fallen asleep and prevent any more misunderstandings.

But an even bigger reason was to flee the nagging thought

of what it might be like if the woman's words were true, and there were no nightmares to deal with. No war. And if Sammi was indeed his wife.

CHAPTER ELEVEN

SOMETHING touched her face.

Mark.

Pulling herself from the bottom of a drugged pool, she blinked open her eyes to find her head trapped between two hard surfaces.

She took in her surroundings. White walls, astringent bite that hung on the air, reception desk.

Her glance moved back. Reception desk. She was at the hospital. But why?

Everything came back in a rush. Seeing Hannah trapped in her car, the needle decompressions she'd had to perform.

But that didn't explain why she couldn't move her head.

Then she saw the masculine thigh lying next to her own. Touching it. Her attention moved to her fingers which were wrapped around a muscular biceps.

It really was Mark. His head was lying on top of her cheek, hence the feeling of being pinned in place.

She must have fallen asleep, and then he'd done the same.

Heat rushed to her face, until she realized he probably wasn't aware of what either of them had done. The last thing she remembered was him talking in hushed tones that had soothed her jangled nerves. All the worry about Hannah and her own exhaustion had just seemed to slide away. She'd relaxed and found herself drifting, following wherever his voice led her.

Her head had dipped a couple of times before settling on a solid perch. Which, evidently, had been his shoulder.

But he was asleep as well, so that was a relief. She could just ease her head from beneath his...

She attempted to do just that, but she really was trapped. If she jerked too hard, he'd wake up with a bump.

Gearing up for another try, he suddenly shifted upright, dragging his hand through his hair.

Pretend you're still asleep? Or let him know you're awake and get it over with?

She voted for the latter, since the continued contact was making her heart lurch around like a drunk on a binge. Sitting up, she rubbed her eyes as if she'd just awoken, feeling like a fraud. But what other choice was there? Just keep on sitting there with her head propped on his shoulder and have him wonder if she was making a move on him?

The thought made her stomach give an ominous twist.

'Looks like we both fell asleep,' she said, thanking her lucky stars her voice was indeed low and scratchy

Glancing across the room, she saw another woman smiling at them. 'Your husband said you were exhausted. But he evidently was as well.'

Husband? Had she done more than drool on his shoulder?

Before she could open her mouth to ask what she meant, Mark said in a low voice, 'It was a little complicated to explain at the time.'

I'll bet.

She forced herself to smile at the older woman. 'It's been quite a night.'

'I think it has been for everyone.' A man showed up behind the older woman and handed her a coat, waiting as she rose to her feet. 'Best of luck with your loved one.'

Okay, this conversation was a little odd. 'Thank you. To you as well.'

The man helped her slip on the coat, then the pair made their way to the door, the woman using a cane to help her progress.

Once they were out of sight, Mark said, 'She assumed…you were asleep. It seemed harmless.'

Harmless. Maybe for him. But having the woman refer to Mark as her husband made something zing through her chest.

A flash of hope?

Surely not. Most probably regret. Regret for her failed marriage. Regret that her son didn't have a live-in father.

Regret that her youthful dreams had been crushed before they'd ever been fully realized.

'It's fine. It's not like we'll ever see them again.' She sat a little straighter. 'Any more news on Hannah?'

'No. It's only been a couple of hours.'

'How long can it take to repair her ribs?'

'Maybe the situation was a little more complicated than they anticipated.'

Panic shot through her stomach.

'Molly said the tear was worse than they expected. There was air leaking into her chest during the flight, but it wasn't filling up with every breath she took.'

Mark put his arm around her and squeezed. 'Let's not jump to conclusions before we know what's going on.' He stood. 'I'm going to run for more coffee, would you like some?'

She shook her head. 'My nerves are on edge enough as it is. It'll just make me jittery, especially this late at night.' Glancing at her watch, she saw that it was only ten-thirty. It felt so much later. 'On second thoughts, if they have some decaf or a cappuccino in the vending machine, I'd accept that. Let me dig out some money.'

'I've got it.' He turned on his heel and headed down the corridor that led to the cafeteria.

Sammi sat back and checked out the waiting room. Still quiet. Sending up a quick prayer that Hannah would come through surgery without any major problems, she toyed with whether or not to call her mom again. She decided against it, worried she might wake Toby. While he was probably out like a light, her mom was a night owl who stayed up until all hours. An old habit ingrained by a husband who'd consistently come home late.

Even though deep down her mother had known their marriage vows had been purely one-sided, she'd stuck with him. She'd asked Mark why his mother had stayed with his father. But Sammi could very well ask herself that same question: why had her mother stayed with someone who'd cheated on her? Sammi's schoolmates had all known who her dad was sleeping with on any given week and had teased her about it. It was one of the reasons Mark's current behavior appalled her so much. He hadn't been like this while they'd been together, never even hinted that he'd wanted to see other people. In fact, at one point she'd been sure he was gearing up to ask her to marry her.

But he hadn't.

And now he couldn't seem to stick with any one woman for very long. What had changed?

He wasn't in a committed relationship, so it technically wasn't cheating, but it seemed wrong to skid from one woman to another, never waiting around to see if things felt right.

She sensed there was more to Mark's actions than met the eye—at least she hoped there was—because he had so many other great qualities. But she felt for the woman who eventually *did* get involved with him. Who fell head over heels for him.

Did she really believe he'd cheat on someone he'd given his word to?

No.

Maybe that's why he'd never given it in the first place. Why he'd left her all those years ago. He'd known he was incapable of being monogamous, so he'd simply never committed.

To anyone.

At least he hadn't put on a front, like her father had…as if he were an upstanding husband and a pillar of the community. Her dad had finally moved on to another wife, and Mark's dad had died of a heart attack just months before Mark had come home. Both women were now free to live their lives as they saw fit.

She spied Mark at the far end of the hallway carrying two paper mugs. His concentration was fastened on the cups, giving her the chance to study him.

Loose-limbed, he moved with ease, his tall build and broad shoulders giving off a kind of steady confidence that turned heads. Dark hair fell over his forehead, long enough to need strong fingers to sweep it back again and again. She could still remember how those silky locks had felt sliding through her own fingertips. A trace of dark stubble now lined his jaw, although he'd been clean-shaven that morning at the plane. And the man made her mouth water as much now as he had when they'd tiptoed from their teenage years and fallen headlong into young adulthood.

Yes, the man was gorgeous, but Sammi was smarter and hopefully wiser now than she'd been all those years ago.

He reached her and handed over a cup. A mountain of foam covered the dark liquid and a dusting of—cinnamon?—lay on top. She eyed it. 'I didn't know the vending machines did cinnamon.'

'They don't. I broke into the kitchen supply cupboard.'

Her eyes widened. 'You didn't!'

'Well, not exactly. I picked the lock.' At her still shocked look, he added, 'Don't worry, I put the container back and re-locked the cabinet.'

Sammi laughed, despite herself, and sipped the coffee. It was rich and luscious and she could just about bet he'd nabbed some flavored creamer from somewhere as well. Her tongue darted out to lick the clinging sweetness from her lips, noting that Mark followed the movement. Her laughter died in her throat.

So he wasn't as immune to her as she'd thought. She didn't

know whether the idea pleased her or terrified her. Scrabbling for something safe to say, she blurted out, 'What did you get?'

He held his cup down so she could see inside. 'Espresso. Black.'

Not a hint of foam, which meant he'd broken into the cupboard just for her. It was a typical Mark thing to do. At least the Mark she'd once known. She willed herself to stay indifferent, but it warmed her from the inside in a way the doctored-up cup of java never could. 'Wow. Espresso. You're going to be up all night. I promise.'

As soon as the words tumbled out, she cringed. She took a deep gulp of her coffee, scalding her tonsils and a good part of her throat in the process. Sucking in a deep breath to ease the burn, she turned toward one of the windows, watching the snow as it blanketed the parking lot and walkways. 'It's coming down faster.'

The heat of his body reached her as he took his seat again. 'I meant to tell you earlier, but with everything else going on I didn't get a chance. A storm front is moving through, with some heavy winds and snow predicted over the next couple of days.'

'Are you kidding me?'

'It's a good thing we got Hannah here when we did, because I doubt the airport will be clear for much longer.'

'It'll be gone by tomorrow, when we need to leave, right?'

He didn't say anything, and she looked into his face, which was lined with something she didn't understand.

'Mark, will we be able to fly home tomorrow?'

'I don't know.'

A spear of panic shot through her. 'I have to get home to my son!'

He hesitated, then used his thumb to brush back a strand of hair that had fallen into her eyes. Something he'd done repeatedly. 'I checked with Toby when we were at the scene of the accident. He said your mom keeps a couple extra inhalers on hand, so he should be fine. We'll call and let her know what's going on. She'll understand.'

She started to relax in her seat then tensed again as another thought hit her.

Toby and her mother might be okay, but what about her? The last thing she needed right now was to be stranded in Anchorage with Mark.

But it looked like that was exactly what was going to happen.

CHAPTER TWELVE

'Heavy snows continue in our area for the next twenty-four to forty-eight hours, delaying flights and making roads impassable.'

Sammi rolled over in bed at the hotel and groaned at the forecaster on TV. Yes, she knew winter was closing in on them—and brutal storms often blew into Alaska with little notice—but couldn't it have waited until she got back home? Maybe if they'd flown out right away, they could have reached Dutch Harbor before it hit.

But Mark had said he didn't like to fly back and forth in one day.

Besides, she'd needed to know how Hannah was doing.

Molly had come out three hours after surgery had started and said the PA was in Recovery. Her rib and lung had been patched up, and she was not in pain at the moment.

Sammi had gone back and held Hannah's hand as she'd slowly emerged from the effects of anesthesia.

'How are you doing, kiddo?' She'd sensed Mark standing slightly behind her, but had forced herself to keep her attention focused on her friend.

'I feel like someone stabbed me with every needle in their arsenal.'

Sammi had smiled. 'That would be me. We had to deflate all that hot air you were storing.'

'Gee. Thanks.' She'd shifted in bed, wincing as she did. 'They put a U-plate on my rib to hold it in place, so it doesn't wander back into my lung. Looks like I'll be stuck here for a week or so.'

'You deserve some vacation time, anyway.'

'Some vacation. Are you going to be okay?'

'Sure.' She leaned down and kissed her cheek. 'Lynn and I can hold the fort until you're better.'

'But—'

'Don't worry about tomorrow, because today has enough worries of its own. Wasn't that the quote you taped to the clinic wall, right behind the reception desk?'

Hannah nodded. 'My daddy was a preacher. Some of it stuck.'

'He was right. You've got plenty to keep you busy for today and the next several days. Just concentrate on healing.'

Her thoughts returned to Mark, even as the meteorologist continued relaying storm warnings in the background. She scowled, throwing back the covers and climbing from the cocooning warmth of her bed. Why was he always right at the periphery of her mind?

Because he's flying you back to Dutch Harbor, you ninny.

She dragged herself to the bathroom, her frown deepening as she looked at herself. She'd had to sleep in the buff, since she hadn't brought any extra clothes, but at least the panties she'd washed out by hand seemed dry enough. Her hair was an absolute rat's nest…and that was currently her best feature. Not a good sign. Just because she was stranded it didn't mean she could hide out naked for the next day or so.

She dragged on her clothes, which were wrinkled both from sitting on the plane and from the wait at the hospital. Maybe she could run the hotel's blow-dryer over them and relax the worst of the creases. Besides, the warm air would be a welcome change from the constant chill the storm had dragged with it. Once she washed her face and scrubbed her teeth as best she could with a washcloth, she undid her braid. It was still damp from her shower last night. Better to leave it down until it dried out some more. As she was brushing the tangles out, her stomach gave an angry rumble.

Food.

Do you still have that candy bar from last week stuffed in your purse?

She went to the other room and rummaged around for a minute or two, but the chocolate had mysteriously vanished. Stolen. Um, yeah. Probably by her own hand. The hotel had a couple of vending machines if she remembered right, so she wouldn't starve. She just had to get up the nerve to venture out in the snow.

Someone knocked on the door, and she froze.

The sound came again, this time accompanied by a voice. 'Sam? If you're in there, could you open up? It's freezing out here.'

Mark. Who else would it be?

She hurried to the door and found him standing hunched in his coat, snowflakes sticking to his hair. His arms were full of bags. She realized she was just staring at him when his brows went up in question.

'Oh, for heaven's sake. Sorry. Come in.' She stood to the side and let him through the door. 'What is all that?'

'Food. Toothbrushes. Stuff.'

Had the man read her mind?

She took several of the packages from him, noticing he also had two coffee cups tucked into the crook of his elbow. Fragrant steam wafted from beneath the lids. Tossing everything else onto the bed, she rescued what she considered to be the most precious commodity right now.

'Um, you might want to be careful with some of those.' But as she sniffed first one cup and then the other to see which held a whiff of vanilla creamer, he smiled. 'I thought that might hit the spot.'

She gave what she hoped was a nonchalant grunt as she peeled back the tab on top of the cup and took a cautious sip, groaning in ecstasy. 'Mmm…still so hot.'

'I assume you're referring to the coffee and not to me.' He shook the moisture from his hair and raked his fingers through it a couple of times. 'Although I think I deserve a bone for braving this weather to make sure your pearly whites stay clean and cavity-free.'

Heat washed over her face. Okay, so the man was still hot as well, even with a nose that was red from the cold, but no way was she going to admit that out loud. Especially since he did in one sweep of his hand what had taken her at least twenty minutes to do: restore order to his hair. 'The coffee has earned you something. And if you have a Boston cream donut in one of those bags, you're getting extra points for sure.'

A slow smile appeared on his face, and he shrugged out of his coat, tossing it onto one of the chairs next to a minuscule table. He seemed awfully chipper this morning. Maybe he'd gotten a better night's sleep than she had.

Sorting through the bags, he pulled out a napkin and then opened a box. He soon had cradled within his palms a perfect round disk of pleasure, its chocolate icing in pristine condition. 'It's fresh. I made sure.'

Sammi gulped, the caffeine hitting her system and sparking a rush of emotions…giddiness being one of the first she recognized.

No grabbing.

Instead she reached out and gingerly took the offering from him with a sniff. 'I'll be the judge of that.' She bit into the donut and the powder-soft dough was indeed extremely fresh. Probably made just minutes earlier. As hard as she tried, she couldn't suppress yet another moan as the vanilla cream center mixed with the warm chocolate frosting.

'I take it the verdict is in?'

She nodded, her mouth full of donut and her heart squeezing

with happiness. She gave a thumbs-up sign the best she could with her hand still wrapped around the coffee cup.

Mark took a donut of his own, simple glazed, and bit into it, taking a seat at the table. Okay, so was it too much to expect for him to leave the box of donuts and venture back into the storm to go to his own room?

Of course it was. She set her coffee on the table across from him and took the other seat. The one with Mark's coat draped across the back. The chill of icy raindrops penetrated her thin cotton top. Despite the moisture, the scent of Mark's body clung to the leather, and she just wanted to pull it around her shoulders.

'Sorry,' he said, retrieving the coat and hanging it on the hook behind the door.

'It's okay.' She gave a deep sigh. 'Thanks for bringing this. I didn't realize how hungry I was.'

Well, it was only a tiny lie.

Mark reached over and grabbed the box of donuts and put the whole thing in front of her. Donuts of every shape and size met her glance. 'Oh my gosh. I'm going to gain ten pounds.'

'Doubtful. Besides, you work hard enough to burn off those calories and more.'

'A nice thought, but not true.' She glanced at the rest of the packages. 'Surely you didn't bring more food.'

'Nope. Just the stuff that's bad for you.' He glanced over as well. 'I thought you might like a toothbrush. I know I would.'

Her brows shot up. 'You needed three bags to carry two toothbrushes?'

'No, I also brought you a book. I wasn't sure what you'd like so I guessed.' He paused and glanced away. 'I also got a little something for Toby.'

'Toby?' She blinked at him, her mind running through the dates, horrified that she might have forgotten something crucial. 'His birthday isn't until next month.'

'It's nothing big. I just saw it and thought he might like it.'

Sammi's gaze went to the window out front. The snow was piled deep, although the parking lot had already seen the blade of a snowplow. 'You drove in this?'

'It's not as bad as it looks, actually.'

Hope flared in her chest. 'So we might make it out of here today?'

His lips twisted. 'Sorry. Driving in it and taking off in it are two different things. The worst of the storm is still out over the ocean. We'd have to fly right through it, not something I particularly want to do.'

'Oh.' She sagged back in her seat, nibbling her donut.

'I did bring some playing cards, if you're interested.'

Sammi's heart stopped for a minute before taking off at a gallop. Their game had been poker. And they hadn't played for money. 'Um…'

How exactly did you ask what seemed to be an obvious question? Was this regular poker or the naughty kind?

'I seem to remember always losing.' His innocent blink did nothing to quell her suspicions.

He had indeed. Repeatedly. At first, Sammi had thought it was because she was an awesome player. Later, she'd realized he stayed one step ahead of her so she wouldn't be the one who shed the last piece of clothing at the end. He hadn't wanted her to be embarrassed. Although he'd seen every inch of her body by then. And she'd traced every contour of his with her fingertips. In fact, they'd rarely made it to the end of a game.

Not a good memory to dwell on when she was currently in a hotel room all alone with the man.

Time to be evasive. 'I haven't played cards in a long time. I've probably forgotten how.'

A brow quirked up. 'Really? Is it possible to forget?'

What was with him? She couldn't imagine him wanting to take a trip down memory lane. Especially since he was the one who'd run away from it in the first place.

'Yes. It is possible. And sometimes it's better not to pick up old habits.'

Zing! That should have earned her a point or two. And sent him a message that she wasn't looking to heat things up between them.

Liar. She might not be looking to, but she was definitely warmer than she'd been before he'd shown up at her door.

He closed the top on the box of the donuts, and Sammi imagined he was also closing the lid on this particular conversation.

'So what do we do until the storm passes?' she asked.

'I offered a simple game of cards, but you shot that down. I'm all out of options.'

The cellphone on the end table went off, the vibration sending the thing careening toward the edge. She hurried over and grabbed it before it fell. Glancing at the screen, she swore softly. Just what she needed.

'Hello?'

'Samantha? Where the hell are you? I've been calling the house since yesterday afternoon.'

Brad. And he was not happy.

'Why didn't you call my cell?'

'That's what I'm doing now.' Her ex's voice was tight and angry, which was unusual for him.

'Sorry. I had a medevac yesterday, and I'm having to stay in Anchorage because of the storm. Don't worry, I haven't forgotten that you have Toby next weekend.'

'You're in Anchorage? You told me you weren't doing medevacs any more.'

'Molly got married, remember? We talked about this.'

'I still don't like it. And what is our son going to do, while you're gallivanting around?'

Gallivanting around?

A knot of anger twisted in her gut. She glanced at Mark and then away, embarrassment crawling over her. Brad's phone voice tended to be twenty times louder than his normal speaking voice, so Sammi had to hold the cell slightly away from her ear. No doubt Mark could hear every word the man said. 'Toby's staying with my mother.'

'You couldn't have brought him with you? He could have stayed with Maribel and me. At least he'd be with *one* of his parents.'

The knot tightened. 'I was with a patient, Brad. Car accident. It wouldn't have been the best thing for Toby to witness.'

There was a moment of silence. 'If you're going to be away from home a lot, maybe we should rethink this custody thing. Make it a more even split. I talked to Maribel, and she wouldn't mind having Toby around more often. Wouldn't it be better for him to be a part of a *whole* family? It's not good for him to be shuffled from person to person. Especially with his condition. What if he has an attack, and you're not there?'

Her growing fury morphed into terror in a split second. He'd hit on the very thing she feared the most. That Toby would need her and she wouldn't be there.

But to change their custody agreement? She'd never in a million years thought Brad would want to go there. Toby was all she had. Brad had his own family now. Would he really try to take their son away from her?

She knew she was overreacting, but couldn't seem to stop herself.

Brad's voice came back over the line. 'Toby needs stability. He needs to know at least one of his parents will be there at all times.'

'You travel, sometimes, too.' Her words tumbled over themselves. *Breathe. Do not let him rattle you.*

'Yes, but Maribel would be here. And Jessica. He'd be able to stay at home. Attend a good school.'

'His school is fine. And my mother is a wonderful caregiver.'

Brad's volume went up another decibel. 'Your *mother* hasn't always made the best choices, though, has she? What if she gets involved with another sleazebag like your father? Is that really who you want Toby to be around? The example you want him to see?'

Oh, God. Mark's eyes had narrowed, zeroing in on hers. Something dark and angry lurked below the surface.

'Can we please discuss this later? I—I'm not alone.'

A poisonous silence lit up the line between them, and she realized how her words might have sounded.

'What do you mean you're not alone?' The words were shouted so loudly, her ear rang, even with the phone held a couple inches away. 'I thought you flew in with a *patient*? If I find out you left Toby in Unalaska so you could—'

Before Brad could finish his sentence, Mark strode across the room and took the phone from her hand, her ex's voice still raging in the background. Pressing the phone to his ear, he said, 'Brad, this is Mark.'

Unlike Sammi, he evidently had no problem absorbing Brad's full volume directly into his ear canal. All she heard was the mumble of her ex-husband's voice, but his outrage came through loud and clear.

Mark's answering smile held a tinge of cruelty as he answered. 'I'm the medevac pilot who flew Sammi and her patient into Anchorage. I'd advise you to dial back the accusations. This isn't doing anyone any good. You can call the hospital and check with them, if you don't believe her. You, more than anyone, should know that Sammi doesn't lie.'

Although Mark's voice was low and even, there was an undercurrent of steel running through it, and a muscle spasmed in his jaw. He was furious. For her.

Sudden warmth bloomed in her stomach and flowed to parts that had frozen over when Brad had suggested he might fight her over custody. She sagged onto the bed, relief washing over her. There was something primitive about the way Mark handled Brad, like a sleek, lethal cat who had no qualms about dealing a death blow if crossed.

She could no longer hear Brad at all, but he'd apparently taken Mark's advice and toned down the threats, because after a moment or two the conversation ended.

Mark set the phone back on the end table and stared at it for a second or two. 'Bastard.'

Biting her lip, she wasn't sure what to say, but he evidently wasn't done talking, because he went on, 'You don't have to put up with that, you know.'

'He's not normally like that. Besides, he's Toby's father. I should have called to let him know where I'd be, but I forgot.' She had. With all the stuff that had gone on with Hannah, notifying Brad had completely slipped her mind.

Mark sat on the bed next to her, his fingers going to her chin and forcing her to look at him. 'I don't know what happened between the two of you during your marriage, but I don't like him yelling at you—accusing you of things that aren't true.' His eyes bored into hers, anger and something else pulsing in their depths. 'I have to ask, Sam. Did it ever go further than that? Further than yelling? Further than empty threats?'

'I—I'm not sure what you mean.'

His fingers tightened fractionally, not allowing her to pull from his grip. 'Sammi, did that man ever raise a hand to you? To Toby?'

CHAPTER THIRTEEN

PROTECT and Defend.

Those words had been drilled into him as a new recruit. And they echoed what he'd tried to do his entire life. First with his mom, and then with his buddies in the service. Finally with Ahmed, who had lain dying in the back of his chopper.

And now with Sammi.

But as soon as he saw the dismay on her face, he realized he'd overstepped his bounds.

'If you're asking if he hit us, no. Never. How could you think I'd ever allow *anyone* to put Toby in danger? Or myself?' Her shoulders relaxed, and she gave a small smile. 'I can take care of myself, so no need to go all caveman on me.'

Caveman.

His fingers gentled on her chin, and he smiled back. Okay, so maybe he had overreacted. As he stared at her, something inside him shifted, and his fingers left her chin to trace across her cheek, gently tucking her hair behind her ear.

'I like your hair down.' He rubbed the strands between his fingers, the satiny texture whispering against his skin. 'It's softer than anything I've ever felt.'

'Thank you.' Her tongue swiped at her lower lip, leaving it moist and inviting. 'I...'

The words died away as if she'd seen his eyes follow the movement.

She was so beautiful. So incredibly strong.

'Sam…' Unable to resist any longer, his head lowered, mouth touching hers, seeing if she'd allow it—if she'd feel the need to defend herself against him.

She held completely still.

And he…hell, he couldn't stop the surge of emotions that erupted within him—neither could he seal the bevy of cracks that appeared in the concrete wall encircling his heart. The wall he'd cemented shut the second his father had uttered that obscure threat against Sammi. He'd reinforced that barrier when he'd learned she'd gotten married…had had a child with someone else. But her kiss had just blown the cover off, exposing every hope and fear he'd shoved inside.

Sammi's hands went to his shoulders, and he could have sworn it was with the intent of pushing him away, but instead they curled into his shirt and hung on, tugging him closer.

The fingers that had touched her hair now tunneled beneath the shiny locks, his palm cupping the back of her head and holding her close as his mouth increased its pressure.

Ahhh…hell.

He relaxed into the swirling sensations, telling himself he could stop any time he wanted.

No, that was a lie. He couldn't stop. Not yet.

His tongue moved along the seam of her mouth, licking across her lower lip, tasting the last traces of sugar from the donut she'd eaten earlier. A shudder rippled through her, and her mouth opened, inviting him in.

There was no hesitation, only action, and he slid home with a low growl of need. The blood rushed to his head and immediately pumped back down into other areas, filling…swelling.

How could a simple kiss do that?

Because nothing was simple where Sammi Trenton was concerned. She provoked emotions that were complex—that ran deeper than anything he'd ever experienced. And he'd stayed away for eight long years.

Almost long enough to forget how it had been with her. The release he'd found in her arms.

Almost. But not quite. And this woman could touch him in ways no other ever had. And he'd been damned glad of it. At least that's what he'd told himself.

So why now?

Forget it. You can figure it out later.

Mark's other hand came up and cupped her jaw, his thumb strumming along its length before moving to where their mouths were fused together, needing tangible evidence of what was happening between them.

The sensation was erotic, crazy, and when the tip of her tongue darted out to slide over the pad of his finger a blast of need ricocheted through his skull. The subtle friction put all his nerve endings on high alert. She coaxed his thumb inside her mouth, abandoning his lips in order to fully wrap around his digit, her tongue swirling over it before sucking it deeper.

'*Sam*.' The word whispered against her mouth was low and tortured. A half-hearted plea for her to stop.

Except she didn't. And the soft moan that met his ears said she was as lost in the moment as he was.

Enough of this. He eased his thumb from her mouth, sliding its wetness across her lips before he claimed them again, his kiss no longer gentle.

Something tugged at the bottom of his shirt, freeing it from the waistband of his jeans, then her hands were on his skin, sliding up and over before splaying across his chest. The slight coolness of her palms did nothing to cool his ardor. In fact, all it did was make him pull her closer, trapping her hands between their bodies. He didn't want them wandering to other areas. Not when he was still drinking in the luscious sensation of her mouth on his, her tongue cradled against the curve of his. She could do all the exploring she wanted to. Later.

Angling his head to the left, he somehow managed to get

closer, although he wasn't sure how. He could have sworn a second ago that was impossible.

He itched to touch her, and found his hands wandering from the back of her head to her shoulders, and then down her arms, the soft shirt she wore keeping him from skin to skin contact. He glided lower, encountering the lower band of the garment, which, unlike his own, wasn't tucked into her slacks.

Don't do it.

His body ignored that command completely, pulling back just enough so his fingers could tunnel beneath the shirt, his breath imprisoned in his lungs as he waited for her reaction.

It only took a second. The tiny whimper…the press of her body into his hands. He wrapped his fingers around her rib cage, his thumbs exploring the long, lean bones before moving higher to the place where her bra met the warmth of her skin.

He swallowed, forcing himself to stay there, rather than move any higher, his mouth going to the line of her neck. Nibbling, tasting.

Biting.

'Oh.' Her breathy sigh only heightened his senses, bringing them to a frenzy of want, need…and something he shied away from. Instead, he concentrated on the here and now. The sound of her breathing, the sweet scent of her bare skin beneath his lips.

As if she suddenly realized her hands were free to roam, they crept to his shoulders, sliding over them, her fingers pressing into his flesh—he wasn't sure of the reason, but he liked it.

Things seemed to move fast forward, and what he'd been satisfied with a minute earlier became a gnawing discontent that ate at him. Tempted him to leap ahead. The second her fingertips slid across his nipples, an arc of electricity went through him before settling in his groin, which was already pulsing with impatience.

He came back up and covered her mouth with his. 'Slow.'

His plea went unanswered and her fingers left their perch, moving in a beeline toward his…

Catching her hands just before she reached the danger zone, he imprisoned them, easing her back onto the bed and leaning over her. He stared into her eyes, huge dark pupils meeting his own.

'Say no,' he whispered, some sane part of him still looking for an escape.

Her throat moved, then she slowly shook her head. 'I can't.'

'You can't do this? Or you can't say no?'

As much as his mind wanted her to answer the former, his heart wanted something far different. But he had to hear the words—to know for sure. If she didn't want him, he'd find the strength to let her up. Even as the thought went through his head, his hands tightened on her wrists.

'I…'

Her lips parted as if she was battling something inside herself. Then, instead of answering, she raised her head and drew her tongue from the base of his throat all the way up to his chin, a slow deliberate move that told him everything he needed to know.

The world swirled around him in slow motion, then he sat up and dragged his shirt over his head, his mind already on his wallet, hoping he had something inside.

Sammi's fingers immediately trailed over his nipples again before they moon-walked down his abs. His stomach muscles rippled in that half ticklish, half tormented sensation that skated the line between eroticism and…

Oh, sweet Jesus.

She'd reached his waistband and flipped open the button in a quick move that left him breathless.

'Sam.' He injected a hint of warning into his voice and lifted her hands above her head, pressing them into the mattress and holding them there for a second or two to emphasize his point. 'Don't move.'

When he let her go, she stayed right where he'd placed her, and a feeling of power flowed through him. Until she arched her back slightly, her lips curving in a smile that turned the tables in an instant.

His fingers again went to the bottom of her blouse, but this time, instead of sliding beneath it, he pulled the garment up and over her head, until she was free of it. He wrapped one of his hands around her wrists, making sure she stayed put as his eyes roamed over the bared flesh before him.

Her lacy black bra played peek-a-boo with her breasts, giving hints of where the rosy center met pale white flesh. Her flat stomach rose and fell in time with her quickening breaths, and she squirmed a bit beneath his gaze. He splayed his hand across her lower tummy, amazed at the difference between them, his rough, tanned skin, her soft white curves.

Unable to wait, he palmed her breast, loving the way it filled his hand to perfection, the way she rose to meet his touch. He released her, undoing the front hook on her bra and slowly easing it away until she lay exposed…her gorgeous body a work of art.

Kissing her mouth, then pressing his lips against her throat, he made his way down until he reached his goal, her quick gasp heightening his pleasure as he suckled first one breast and then the other.

Her hands left the pillow and slid down his sides, and he didn't stop her this time when she reached his zipper. The tab inched its way down as she wrestled with it, stopping a time or two when he employed his teeth, holding her in place while his tongue lapped over her. Dark mutterings mixed with sighs until she finally had the zipper undone. She soon had him in her palm and his body tightened to the point of pain.

Too soon.

He wouldn't last much longer at this rate. Lifting his head, he went to work on her own jeans, surprised by how unsteady his hands were. He'd never had a problem before. He released the snap and tugged the slacks over her hips until she helped him kick them off the rest of the way.

Panties next. They matched her bra, and he fingered the elastic for a few seconds knowing once this final barrier was removed it was all over. There'd be no going back.

'Are you sure?'

Her response was to bat his hands away and push the garment down her legs, making short work of them. Once she was naked, her delicate brows arched. 'I think it's your move, fly boy.'

He gave a low laugh. The woman he'd known as a girl had always waited for him to take the lead. He'd stayed one step ahead of her in their card games for just this reason. There was no longer any need. She'd grown into a witch who knew exactly what to do to drive him crazy. He suppressed the slight flare of jealousy that someone else had led her to this point.

Your fault.

He'd chosen to leave, no matter what the reasons, therefore he had no say as to how she lived her life. 'I have to check something first.'

He didn't bother to cover himself, and as he wrestled his wallet from his back pocket she ran her index finger down his exposed flesh, making it—and him—jump.

Be in here, dammit. He flipped open his billfold and checked the tiny compartment. *Success.*

There was only one, though, so he'd better make this count.

He tossed the condom onto the bed, standing on the floor to rid himself of the rest of his clothes. When he came back down, covering her with his body, the shock of her flesh against his made his pulse run wild. He kissed her, his hand sliding between their bodies to the heart of her, finding moist heat. Ready. All he had to do was slide home…

Not quite yet.

Continuing to kiss her, he gritted his teeth and stroked her, swallowing her moans, murmuring nonsensical phrases that meant nothing…and everything.

'Mark.' The whispered word carried a plea he gladly heeded.

Ripping open the square packet and sheathing himself, he nudged her knees apart, settling between them with a muttered threat to his own body which was screaming for release.

He surged forward, the tightness he found almost pushing him over the edge. When she tried to lift her hips he used his weight to hold her in place. 'Shh. Just give me a minute.'

'Mark…no…I…' Her body bucked against his.

At first he thought she was fighting him, that she'd changed her mind, then realized she was right on the brink. He gave up trying to hold on and let go, meeting her thrust for thrust as she arched and retreated, her head twisting from side to side.

She stiffened, with him buried deep inside her, eyes flying open to fasten on his just as her body gave way to a series of glorious spasms that catapulted him into the stratosphere. He groaned as he pumped into her, riding out his own release, until he was empty.

No, not empty.

Full. Like he'd never been in his life. Like he'd never dreamed he *could* be.

Gathering her to him, he rolled onto his side, carrying her with him, relishing the slight sheen of moisture that covered her body, the breathlessness as she buried her head in the crook of his neck.

He swallowed hard, a sudden wetness appearing behind his eyes that he didn't understand. Was afraid to explore.

It had to be the stress of the flight. The emotional tension that came with Hannah's injury followed by that phone call. He'd soon feel like he did with every other woman. A physical release that began and ended there.

Except he'd never carried more than one condom in his wallet, because he'd never felt the need to stage an instant replay.

Until now.

He and Sammi had just expended violent amounts of energy in a short period of time. Instead of feeling replete and sleepy, he wanted her again. Was already hardening within her—the temptation to just say to hell with it all and take her despite the risks.

And that terrified him.

He'd lived the past several years in a way that kept any explosive emotions under a tight leash. Contained within an iron fist.

He was never out of control. *Never.*

Until now.

CHAPTER FOURTEEN

'THERE you go, Sarah. A little bandage and you're all set.'

Sammi smoothed the adhesive edges of the large square gauze pad on the child's forearm, which covered six brand new stitches. They looked kind of like the set Sammi now sported across the center of her heart. Six days and counting since she'd returned to Dutch Harbor after her disastrous encounter with Mark. The storm had let up unexpectedly, and they'd been able to fly out that day after all. Thank God!

She'd sworn she'd never fall at his feet like the legions of other women he'd been with. And yet she'd toppled like a sapling in a hurricane after he'd picked up that phone and tried to defend her honor. At his concern for her well-being.

'Will it leave a scar?' the girl's mother asked, bringing Sammi back to the present with a bump.

'Probably a little one. Make sure you keep the sun off the new skin as it heals. Either cover it with a bandage whenever you're outside or load it down with a good-quality sunscreen, once the stitches come out.'

Sarah, who'd surprised both women by not uttering a peep during the administration of the anesthetic or during the stitching itself, said, 'Now Johnny Riker can't say he's the only one with a battle car.'

Her mom smiled. 'I think you mean *scar*.'

'Huh? You mean I don't get a car?' The six-year-old crossed her arms over her chest and scowled.

Becky sighed. 'Nothing prissy about my daughter.'

'That's quite all right. I wasn't either when I was her age. I'm still not.' Sammi forced a smile.

The same age as her son, Sarah had her whole life in front of her. She could be anything she dreamed, do anything she wanted. Well, maybe not drive a 'battle car'.

Actually, an armored vehicle didn't sound like a bad idea right now. She needed something with dark bulletproof glass, so Mark wouldn't see how their time together had affected her. He was used to the whole love 'em and leave 'em philosophy, but she wasn't. She'd been with exactly two men in her life. Mark and her ex-husband. She had no experience to draw from.

Maybe he'd just keep on avoiding her, and they could all get back to their normal lives.

Except he was still the medevac go-to for the foreseeable future. And Sammi wanted nothing more than to have him go back to hauling tourists.

Liar. She wanted something else entirely, but that was never going to happen. Not with a man like Mark.

Okay, enough! You are not *going to spend all day mooning over him.*

Sammi went to the cupboard and pulled down a big glass jar filled with colorful lollypops. Setting it on the counter, she spun it around until the hand-written list of ouchies came into view. Each ailment had a color-coded pop to go with it. It wasn't a perfect system, by any means, but it made the kids feel special.

If only there was a color for her particular boo-boo. Maybe she should add a new one to the bottom of the list. Except there were no more colors available. She should check to see if there were licorice-flavored suckers. Then she could hand one to Mark to go along with his black heart.

Not his fault, Sammi. It takes two.

She went over and helped Sarah hop off the exam table. 'You've earned a treat. You've got a big choice in front of you. See the list here?'

Sarah nodded. 'Red—valor, green—broken bones, yellow—sunny disposition, purple—vac…vac…'

'Vaccinations.'

'Purple—vaccinations, Orange—courage, Blue—stitches.'

What to call the yellow pops had stumped her, until Lynn had suggested putting a positive spin on it. 'See? You have quite a decision to make.'

The child glanced down at her arm. 'I think my stitches will last longer than my courage.'

Sammi knelt in front of her, thanking her lucky stars she'd refilled the popular blue suckers. 'You know, I don't think that's true. I think bravery is something you either have or you don't. You definitely have it.'

Unlike she herself, who was displaying all the hallmarks of a coward.

After that, the choice was easy. Sarah picked orange.

She leaned the jar toward the child and let her retrieve the candy herself. 'As you can see, there are a lot of orange suckers left. Not too many kids are as brave as you.'

After hugging the child, she sent the pair on their way. She started to put the lid back on the lollypop jar but stopped, reaching in to grab an orange lollypop of her own. Maybe the candy itself could infuse her with a dose of courage.

The waiting room was empty, a strange sight. She glanced at Lynn, who shrugged. 'It's a rare sunny day. People evidently have better things to do than get sick or injured.'

'I think I'll go see how Mrs. Litchfield is doing, then. Can you call, if anyone comes in?' The pianist she'd seen a couple of weeks back had been to Anchorage for a consult with the rheumatologist, and Sammi wanted to see if the new medication was helping control her symptoms.

'Are we talking *patients*?' Lynn asked, answering her original question. 'Or are we talking *anyone*?'

Sammi knew exactly who the receptionist was referring to, but chose to ignore it. 'Patients. Anyone else can wait.'

She hurried to her car, wondering if she should call first. But Mrs. Litchfield had told her to drop by whenever she had some spare time, which had been almost nil. Hannah had been in the hospital for almost a week now, which meant Sammi had been pulling double duty. She needed a breath of fresh air.

Pulling up to a stop sign at the end of the road, she watched another car pull up in the opposite direction. Her eyes widened.

Mark's car. Of all the dumb luck.

She scooched down in her seat, realizing how ridiculous it was. He knew what kind of vehicle she drove. Plus, it was kind of hard to steer when you couldn't see a thing.

She started across the road, noting he hadn't moved. Tempted just to bolt past, she tensed when his window started down. It was either be rude or do the same.

Rude sounded good. Really good, but her foot came off the gas and her finger hit the power window button.

But you are not going to be the first one to talk!

'Hey,' she said. Okay, so that orange sucker was kicking in at just the wrong moment. Great.

'Hey, yourself.' Mark paused, his eyes trailing over her face in a way that made the interior of the car turn warm, despite the puff of mist her breath gave off. 'I've been meaning to call, but I've had tourists this week. Are you okay?'

Okay?

Ah, he meant after their fateful encounter. If he was asking if she was so destroyed by their one-night stand that she'd jump off a bridge, she could reassure him she was quite safe.

'I'm fine. Why wouldn't I be?'

There! That should put any fears to rest.

Thank God she had *not* been waiting around by her phone. And since Toby's dad had visitation tomorrow, she'd have to catch the ferry this afternoon. Despite Mark's earlier offer, he probably wanted to be with her even less than she wanted to be with him.

He nodded, his eyes narrowing on her face. 'When's Toby's next trip to the mainland?'

She blinked. Had he read her mind? What now? Lie? Or tell the truth.

Mark had once told her she was a terrible liar, so better just to get it over with. 'His dad is meeting us at the dock to-morrow.'

She glanced in the rear-view mirror to make sure no one was behind her, the chilly air beginning to permeate the car.

'I thought we had a deal.' His voice was so low she had to strain to make out the words, but even so, she knew better than to think he was taking her announcement in his stride. His tone was identical to the one he'd used on the phone with Brad.

Before she could respond, he took a deep breath, seeming to fight for composure, his hands white on the wheel. 'You've bought tickets for the ferry?'

'Not yet, but—'

'Then don't. I'll take you.'

'But your tourists…'

'I flew them back yesterday. I have the weekend off.'

Her brain worked to find another excuse, but came up empty. 'Oh. But I thought…'

'You thought what?' His eyes bored into hers.

She shook her head, unwilling to say it aloud, terrified she'd burst into tears if she even tried.

Suddenly Mark's car door clicked open, and he unlatched his seat belt.

Panic welled up in her throat as he stepped from the vehicle. *What on earth?*

He hadn't bothered putting on a coat, but crossed the space between them, placing his hand on the top of her car and bend-ing down to look inside. 'Did you think I wouldn't want to take you to Anchorage any more after what happened on Sunday?'

'I…I…assumed it would be easier this way.'

'You assumed wrong.' Mark bent closer, his scent carried to her on a stray current of air. It was warm and familiar, and she thought she'd never be rid of it after their time together. 'It's not easier.'

The intensity of the words sent a shiver over her, even though she had no idea what they meant.

His hand came off the door frame and cupped the back of her head. He stared at her for a long moment before leaning through the window and meeting her lips in a hard kiss.

The surge of need was immediate, flooding her system and overflowing the flimsy barriers she'd tried to erect. A soft sound came from her throat. When his fingers tangled in her messy French braid, his tongue seeking entrance, her breath caught in her lungs.

The kiss was abrupt, harsh, like something he'd tried to keep himself from doing and failed. That alone caused her mouth to open, allowing him in. Because she'd done the same thing. Tried to act indifferent…nonchalant, but her insides were a seething cauldron, emotions bubbling to the surface and sinking back down. And as hard as she fought it, at his touch the tension hissed from her in a tight stream, like a balloon that was stretched to its limit.

Had she put the car in neutral? She wasn't sure and at the moment she didn't care. He invaded her mouth the same way he invaded whatever space he inhabited. And she welcomed the assault, tried to force her way past the barrier of the door, only to have her seat belt restrain her.

Then it was over. He backed off, her lips humiliatingly following his for a half-second longer.

He gave a low laugh that rumbled through her chest as he took a step backward. 'No, it's not easier. Not by a long shot.'

* * *

The nightmares had gotten worse, and it was all Sammi's fault. Because they'd gone from nightly reruns of seeing that boy die on his plane to watching a Jeep Sammi was driving hit an IED, shattering into a thousand pieces as he watched it happen in slow motion.

And that IED represented him and his current stupidity. He'd already hurt her once, did he really want to do it again? Mark was no longer the kid he'd once been. The war had marked him. Changed him. And he wasn't sure he could find his way back to 'normal'.

He spent the rest of the day getting his plane ready for their flight, his thoughts a mass of jumbled emotions and regrets. Resting his hand against the metal skin, he shook his head for the hundredth time. He wasn't fit to have a relationship with Sammi or anyone, so kissing her again was tantamount to emotional suicide. But her assurance she was fine and that it was 'easier this way' caused something to snap within him because he'd been through hell and back since their night together, while she'd seemed to have gotten through it with ease.

So that kiss had been as much about seeing her reaction as it had been about needing to touch her again.

Instead of slugging him like the old Sammi might have done, though, she'd made that sexy little sound in the back of her throat and moved into his kiss. The exact same way she'd kissed him when they'd fallen into bed together.

He was screwed. He'd spent the last six months keeping his emotional involvements to a minimum. And he hadn't spent the entire night with a woman in all that time…because he knew what might happen once he fell asleep. There was no way he wanted Sammi—or anyone else—to see him in that condition.

He had to keep his distance.

Kind of hard when you're committed to flying her back and forth so Toby can visit his father.

Oh, hell. That also meant Sammi would be alone in that

hotel room once again. And exactly where did Mark expect to sleep?

He knew one thing for damned sure.

It wouldn't be in Sammi's bed.

CHAPTER FIFTEEN

'You have your inhaler?'

A lump caught in Mark's throat as Sammi leant down to kiss Toby's cheek, tension thick in the air. Sammi had been adamant about meeting Brad at their usual place rather than having her ex meet them at the airport, and Mark had insisted on going with her. If the jerk wanted to accuse them of something, it would be in his presence.

Not that the man would be wrong. They *had* been together. For one night. That didn't mean they were routinely getting it on every time Toby was out of his mother's sight...or that it would ever happen again. Besides, Sammi had mentioned Hannah might catch a ride home with them, if the doctors were ready to discharge her, *and* that she'd be staying in Sammi's hotel room tonight. The inference was that he shouldn't hope for a repeat of their last encounter.

And damn if it hadn't sent a wave of disappointment crashing over him.

Sammi was smart, he had to hand it to her. She wasn't taking any chances that he'd have a relapse and end up back in her bed.

It was for the best. He rolled his eyes. Now, if he could only convince that ticking thing in his chest of that.

Brad gathered Toby's stuff and hustled him off to the car with a curt goodbye that made Mark's shoulders tense.

That tension grew when Sammi turned to him with a bright

smile. 'Well, I guess that's that. I'm off to the hospital to visit Hannah. Shall we meet at the plane tomorrow afternoon for the return flight?'

'How is she?' He ignored the hint that she wanted to get away from him as fast as she could.

'The doctor's going to check her over this afternoon and hopefully release her.'

'Does that seem likely?'

'Unless something changes.' She hesitated. 'She'll still have to rest at home for a few weeks.'

That meant Sammi would still be all alone at the clinic, something he'd hoped wouldn't happen. There were already tell-tale smudges of exhaustion beneath her eyes that would only get worse.

'Can I help?' The words were out before he could stop them.

'What do you mean?'

'How are you going to handle the clinic by yourself?'

'The same way Dr. Stevers used to handle it. It's only for a couple of weeks.'

Was she kidding? Paul Stevers, the general practitioner who'd single-handedly manned the clinic when they'd been kids, had died of a heart attack at age fifty-five.

'You're a mother, Sammi. Is that really fair to Toby?'

She popped her chin into the air, eyes flashing. 'I know exactly what I am. I don't need you—or anyone else—reminding me.'

A clear reference to her argument with Brad last week.

'Hey, I'm sorry.' He took a step closer, his fingers curving around her upper arms to encourage her to look at him. 'I'm worried about you, that's all. I wasn't trying to imply anything about your parenting skills. You've done an awesome job with Toby. Everyone can see that.'

She squinched her nose. 'Ugh. Sorry for snapping. I don't know what's wrong with me.'

'Don't worry about it.' He stroked a finger down the length

of her nose, teasing out the crinkles. 'Listen, why don't you let me take you to the hospital? Afterwards, if Hannah feels up to it, I can take you both out to eat and drop you off at the hotel room. That is, if you don't already have plans.'

'Hannah will still be pretty sore from her surgery, I imagine.' She eased back, forcing him to release her.

The emptiness collecting in his chest was just from the cold air hitting where her warmth had rested. He was almost sure of it. And if Hannah wasn't well enough to leave the hospital or go out to eat, that let him off the hook.

Instead of relief, however, he was filled with a sense of longing he hadn't felt in a very long time.

Not since the day he'd left Dutch Harbor eight years ago.

On Wednesday morning, the red heart on her calendar glared at her from across the kitchen.

'It's only one day,' she muttered, taking her cereal bowl and moving to the two-person dinette.

'What is?' Toby was already there, slurping down the contents of his dish.

'Can we be a little quieter when we eat?' Maybe she could distract him, because no way was she talking to a six-year-old about late periods.

One day.

She'd been late before.

'Sorry.' He proceeded to finish with a little more delicacy until the end, when he held up the bowl with a questioning look.

Sammi laughed. 'Go ahead, since it's the only way I can get you to drink milk.'

Up went the bowl to Toby's lips, where he emptied it. Setting it back on the table, he grinned. 'It tastes like cereal this way.'

Kids were inventive, she'd give them that. If you wouldn't give them chocolate milk to drink in the morning, they'd find a work-around. Human nature never changed.

There was no way she could be pregnant. They'd used a condom. And Mark had pulled away with a rueful grin when she'd reached for him again. A no-more-supplies explanation followed by a quick kiss to the mouth had softened the rejection.

She'd been tempted to chuck caution to the wind, but his actions had been surprisingly responsible, something she might not have given the 'new' Mark credit for. Maybe he wasn't as reckless as he'd seemed in recent months.

The thought wasn't something she wanted to dwell on. It was a whole lot easier to cast him in the role of villain and stay well away from him than to wonder if there were deeper motives for his actions.

For leaving the island all those years ago.

Uh, yeah. He'd wanted to join the military. And he hadn't wanted *her*. That was all she needed to know.

She ate quickly, needing to get Toby off to school and head to the clinic. They were both going to be late if she didn't get a move on.

And what if you are...late? the little voice whispered in the back of her head, renewing the panic she'd awoken to this morning.

Stress.

It wasn't as if she wasn't under a ton of it nowadays. First there had been Toby's asthma attack, then Hannah's accident.

And then there'd been that lovemaking with Mark. World-altering.

Possibly in a more literal sense.

No, it was impossible. She'd taken every precaution.

Actually, Mark had. But she was smart enough to know that one in every fifty condom-alone users would get pregnant. She should have taken some precautions of her own. But she wasn't sexually active.

She still wasn't. So what were the odds?

This is you we're talking about, Sammi. Since when have your odds ever been good? Your mom married a womanizer and then you followed in her footsteps and let yourself get charmed into bed by one.

Except she could swear Mark hadn't done that. He hadn't set out to make her one of his conquests. In fact, after that day in her hotel room, he'd not given any indication that he'd be interested in a repeat. Except for that amazing kiss beside her car last week.

That had flipped her tummy inside out.

It was why she'd asked Hannah to fly back to Dutch Harbor with them. It was a whole lot easier not to send off some kind of weird needy vibes if she had another adult along for the ride.

She sent Toby to brush his teeth while she gathered up the dishes and loaded them in her old rattletrap of a dishwasher that she somehow kept nursing along. It needed to be replaced, as did her refrigerator, but she just didn't have the money. Not with Toby's chronic condition and the co-pay on his inhalers.

And if she was pregnant...

Oh, Lord.

Her hand went to her stomach for a second, shoving back the quick flash of hope. No way did she want Mark's baby. It was crazy thinking.

Was there some kind of stupid gene that could be passed down from mother to daughter?

No, and it wasn't nice to think of her mother in those terms. She'd grown so much since divorcing her father and becoming a grandmother. It seemed she was trying to right all the mistakes of her past. And doing a damned good job of it. Sammi could honestly say she was proud of her mom in a way she'd never been as a teenager or young adult.

You'll start your period tomorrow.

With that positive affirmation ringing in her head, she ran Toby to school then turned her tiny car toward the clinic.

Lynn was already there, as was Hannah.

'What the hell do you think you're doing?' she asked the PA.

'Working?'

'Um…no. You had surgery less than two weeks ago. Car accident…punctured lung…broken rib? Does any of this ring a bell?'

Hannah straightened some charts behind the reception desk, moving slowly and carefully. 'I'm bored out of my skull at home. I need to do something besides dwell on my aches and pains.'

Words Sammi could definitely relate to. She'd been relieved to come to work herself, so she could keep her mind off her own emotional aches and pains.

And if you are pregnant?

What was she going to do about Mark? Tell him?

Uh…yeah. It was the right thing to do. Besides, it wasn't like she was playing leapfrog over the line of guys waiting to take her out. He'd know the baby was his the second she started showing.

She could move away and take Toby with her.

Again, that wouldn't be fair to Mark. She would never keep a child's father from knowing the truth, no matter how awkward things might become. She had no doubt that Mark wanted nothing to do with kids. Why else would he still be single? He was over thirty, and even though that was well within the time range for children nowadays, he didn't seem interested. He'd always seemed kind of uncomfortable around Toby, in fact.

Her hand went unconsciously to her stomach again.

'Are you feeling okay?'

She realized she'd zoned out and that Hannah and Lynn were both staring at her with concerned eyes. 'I'm fine. It's just been a crazy morning.'

Hannah came around the desk and touched her arm. 'I know you've been having to do a lot of extra work, so why don't you take the day off.'

'Didn't we just talk about that broken rib a few minutes ago?'

'I'm fine, just a little tender. Besides, it feels better when I'm on my feet than when I'm sitting down or lying in bed.'

'And if some excited little kid wants to give you a bear hug?'

Hannah's face paled, and Lynn stepped up. 'I'll help with the kids. She can just tell me what to do. I know how to take temperatures and blood pressure. All she has to do is sign her name on the prescription pad. Besides, it's been slow the last couple of days—you said so yourself yesterday.'

Before Sammi could refuse again, the PA insisted, saying, 'Please, Sammi. Let me at least sit behind the desk so I have someone to talk to.' Hannah and Lynn exchanged a meaningful glance.

'I don't know...'

Lynn made a shooing motion with her hands. 'If we get into trouble we'll call someone from the clinic across town. Go have fun while Toby is in school. Or take a nap, whatever sounds good.'

'I think I will, then. Thanks.' She glanced at Hannah. 'I'll have my cellphone, if you need anything.'

'We won't, but thanks.'

The first patient of the day, sporting a cut on her finger, pushed through the double doors and Lynn scooted behind the desk, greeting her and taking down pertinent information. Hannah took Sammi's arm and edged her toward the exit. 'Go before you change your mind. I'll call you if we need you.'

She zipped up her jacket and headed across the parking lot just as Mark pulled up. Her heart lurched, and her steps faltered. Then she sucked down a deep breath and walked over to his car. 'Everything okay?'

'Yep, just wanted to let you know I was flying a pair of tourists over to Umnak. Do you want to come?' He opened the door and got out.

That was strange. Why would he think she was off today?

'Um, I'm not sure I should.'

'Do you have to work?'

'No.'

'So, come with me.' Shoving his hands into the pockets of his jeans, he rocked back on his heels. 'I only have two passengers, so I have some extra room. You could do a little sightseeing. Get away from the clinic for a while.'

'I don't know. I have to be home when Toby gets out of school at four.'

'I told the Parnells I'd have them back by dinner. So that's just about the right time. You could call your mom, if it looks like it's going to be late.'

She hesitated. She hadn't been to Umnak in ages, and she had been putting in a lot of extra hours the last couple of weeks. Sightseeing did sound like fun…and there would be chaperons along for the ride. 'Let me check and make sure she's okay with watching Toby, just in case.'

Mark reached through the window and turned off his engine as she dialed the number. Her mom answered on the second ring.

'Hello?'

'Mom?' Why did this seem so awkward all of a sudden? *Just blurt it out.* 'I'm thinking of flying over to Umnak with Mark and a couple other people. I should be home by the time Toby gets out, but just in case—'

'You're going with Mark?' There was a pause, then her mom's voice came back on the line. 'Oh, that's right. I'd almost forgotten. You should go. I'll be at your house when the Tobeman gets off. If you're already home, maybe we can order a pizza and watch a movie. If you're not, we'll be fine.'

'Are you sure?' Something about her mom's voice made her uneasy. First Mark was acting strangely, and now her mom.

'Of course I am. It's about time you went out with young men your own age.'

'Oh, uh…' She snuck a panicked glance at Mark. 'It's just as friends.'

A slight frown appeared between his brows. Heaven only

knew what he thought her mother had said. It was kind of hard to call them friends after the night they'd spent together two weeks ago. With what might be growing inside her.

She quickly signed off, promising to call her mother if she was late or if their plans changed. To her relief, Mark said nothing once she ended the call.

'Do you want to leave your car here, or should I follow you home?'

Safer to leave the vehicle at the clinic, since her house was empty. She didn't want to go over there, knowing that. Mark might be above temptation, but she, obviously, was not. She was still hopeful her period might start soon, so she already had some supplies tucked into her purse, just in case.

'We can go straight to the airport, if you don't mind dropping me off here when we get back.'

'No problem.'

The pair of tourists was already there when they arrived. Young and obviously in love, the couple held hands and did a whole lot of whispering. That meant Sammi was stuck in the co-pilot's seat, since there was no way the young lovers were going to want to be separated. She sighed as she strapped herself in. As if he knew exactly what she was thinking, Mark gave her a quick smile, one brow lifted in question. 'We're going to do a water landing. One of the boats will meet us in the bay.'

'Why? There's an airstrip on Umnak.'

Mark pushed buttons and pulled levers and glanced back toward his other passengers. She got what he was saying. The customers wanted to see what a real amphibian plane landing was like. Sammi couldn't blame them. If she were in their shoes, she'd probably opt for the same.

'Sounds like fun.' Ha! Then why did her voice sound so glum?

He radioed the tower that they were ready for take-off and got the okay. Taxiing into position, they waited behind another plane, which was next on the line-up. Soon they were in the air, leaving the island behind them.

Flying had always been something Sammi loved, she just didn't get to do it very often. The fact that they could be somewhere in an hour that would have taken three or more by boat still amazed her. So much so that small planes like Mark's didn't faze her.

She stared at the clouds as they passed through them and then leaned over to look at the ocean once they were in the clear. The deep silver water glinted up at her, the whitecaps barely visible from their height. 'It's so beautiful up here. It looks like something out of a movie.'

'I like it too.' His smile was warmer than it had been in recent days. Her system responded with an answering heat.

The man in the back spoke up. 'How long is the flight again?'

'About an hour. Not enough time for our flight attendant to serve drinks, I'm afraid.'

Sammi sent him a glare, thinking at first he meant her, but the passengers' laughter made her realize he was just joking.

Calm down.

'You said the village is small?' The woman, who'd introduced herself as Nancy, asked.

'There are about thirty-nine folks, I think. It's struggling to stay alive, like several of the more remote islands. A lot of the young people have already moved to Anchorage or Unalaska— the island where Sammi and I live. But it's beautiful. The volcano will make some nice background photos.'

The island where Sammi and I live. Those words made an ache settle in her chest. If things had been different, she and Mark could have been like this young couple. Toby could have been…

No. If she and Mark had stayed together, there would be no Toby.

He glanced at her, something dark coming and going in

his eyes. It was almost as if he could read her thoughts. Heat rushed to her face, and she turned to look out the window in case her cheeks were as pink as they felt.

His voice came again. 'There are no cars, so we'll be walking once we're back on land.'

'Understood. Thanks for agreeing to take us.'

'My pleasure.'

Those low words washed over her, and Sammi closed her eyes, pressing her forehead against the icy glass next to her. The chill soon cooled her off enough to face forward again without fearing she'd give herself away.

Despite the awkward silences that fell between the two of them from time to time, the flight passed quickly, and before she knew it they were swooping towards the bay.

Once they landed, the choppy waters rocked the small plane in a quick *one-two...pause* rhythm that she feared might make her seasick, but thankfully she could already see a boat being launched from shore. Someone was waiting for their arrival, just like Mark had said.

He turned to her. 'Once we're on land, do you think you could go somewhere with me? I have an errand to run.'

'An errand?' What could he possibly have to do on the tiny island?

'Yep. I talked to a friend here. She has something I thought Toby might like.' He smiled. 'Don't worry, I've already cleared it with your mother. I promised her I'd make it a surprise.'

CHAPTER SIXTEEN

WOULD she kill him?

Mark sincerely hoped not. He wasn't just doing this for Sammi and Toby, he was also doing it to help a fallen comrade-in-arms. Or at least that comrade's wife.

Sammi's mother—who'd been surprisingly cordial on the phone—had assured him that Toby had always wanted one, and that Sammi had actually looked into the possibility. She just hadn't been able to scrape together the funds yet. So Mark had decided to take matters into his own hands. He just hoped he was doing the right thing in making this trip with her.

The dreams about Sammi had eased over the past week, and he attributed that to the distance he'd kept between them. But he hadn't been able to pass up this opportunity.

If he believed in fate, he might think his father's death meant he and Sammi could finally be together, but it seemed like fate had thrown yet another spanner in the works. It wasn't safe for him to be with Sammi or anyone right now.

No matter how much he might want it.

He'd accepted the fact that this was one woman he'd regret letting slip through his fingers, which was why he'd been very careful to keep recent relationships superficial. Nothing got under his skin nowadays.

Okay, maybe *one* thing. But it was the very thing he couldn't have.

The trip to shore was a little rougher than he'd expected, and he glanced back at his plane, which was still bobbing in place. One of the village men had promised to keep an eye on it and Mark had handed him a walkie-talkie so they could keep in touch, just in case. The villager knew his plans and had already called ahead to let Vonnie know they were on their way.

Sammi sat across the boat, huddled into her coat, looking a bit on the greenish side. He remembered she wasn't a big fan of the water, but she was being pretty stoic about it. She'd leapt onto the dinghy without complaint and had hunkered down in a seat.

He leaned across. 'You okay?'

'Peachy.' Her eyes told a different story. She was wondering what the heck she was doing here. Hopefully she'd soon realize why he'd asked. Even the girls at the clinic had been in on it, making sure Sammi was told in no uncertain terms that she was not welcome at work today. He couldn't believe she'd given in without a fight, though.

The bottom of the boat scraped against shore and the owner got out to drag it a few yards further. Mark glanced at Sammi's feet, relieved to see she had on some sturdy boots. It was one thing he hadn't thought about when he'd planned this crazy outing.

'You two have everything you need?' he asked the pair in the back of the boat.

'Yep. Camera, coffee and a packed lunch.' The man patted his backpack.

'Pick a sheltered spot, since it gets pretty nippy this time of year.' Nippy was an understatement. He and Sammi would be eating at Vonnie's, but he'd given a third walkie-talkie to the pair, telling them to make sure they kept in contact and to call immediately if they got into trouble.

Once off the boat, the lovebirds took off gloved hand in gloved hand, leaving Mark and Sammi alone on the shore.

Sammi shoved her hands into the pockets of her jacket,

glancing with suspicion at his backpack. 'What's this errand you were talking about?'

'I told Vonnie I'd stop in and hang a light for her.'

'Vonnie?' Her brows puckered.

'Donald's sister. You remember him from school?'

'No, I don't… Wait, little Donny Mosely?'

'Yep. His sister moved to Umnak when she got married.'

Her face cleared. 'She's married.'

'Widowed. Her husband died in Afghanistan six months ago, why?' He'd attended his friend's memorial service in Anchorage—one more child left without a father. So many deaths.

'He died? I'm so sorry.' She hesitated. 'I thought you said this trip had something to do with Toby.'

'It does, but you have to promise you're not going to get mad.'

Her feet stopped moving. 'What's going on, Mark?'

'Like I said, it's a surprise.'

Not only did she not start walking again, her hands went to her hips. 'What kind of surprise?'

He took hold of her wrist and started walking, leaving her no choice but to tag along. 'If I told you, it wouldn't be a surprise.'

'I don't even know Vonnie, so I don't understand.'

'If you keep dragging your feet, you're never going to find out, are you?'

'Have I ever told you I hate surprises?'

Did she? That wasn't a good sign. Grace could have told him she might not agree to it before he'd put down a deposit. But if she didn't want it, he'd take it for himself. That way the boy would still get some enjoyment from it, even if it was at Mark's house rather than Sammi's. Although why he thought Sammi would allow Toby to come over was still a little fuzzy in his head.

But at least she was walking next to him willingly, now. Somehow he couldn't bring himself to drop her hand, and she made no move to yank free of his grip. Instead, he threaded his fingers through hers, a strange feeling of rightness again coming over him. He could still remember when he and Sammi had taken walks by the stream in Unalaska, high on the mountain. Just the two of them. And the intimate kisses in the shadow of the salmonberry bushes.

Better not to remember things like that.

They were soon at Vonnie's tiny house and already he could hear sounds of barking coming from the back. The door was flung open, and Vonnie stood in the doorway, her burgeoning abdomen sending a shock wave through him.

She hadn't mentioned being pregnant at the memorial service. It must have happened just before Greg had shipped out. He'd been killed within two months of leaving the States. How terrible that the father would never know the joy of seeing his child's birth.

'Oh.' Sammi's quiet murmur came from beside him, her hand reflexively going to her own stomach.

He swallowed, trying not to put her in Vonnie's place and imagine what it might be like to come home to find her waiting in the doorway, her abdomen just as swollen with child. Except that image soon morphed into that of a young child, who bled out while he watched helplessly.

No kids for him. Not now. Not ever. They were not on his bucket list.

'Mark. You're right on time.' Vonnie's low voice was filled with welcome and a small boy appeared next to her legs. The child couldn't have been older than two or three. 'This is Aaron.'

Mark swallowed hard, trying not to think of Greg or the milestones his friend would be missing in his children's lives. He nodded toward Sammi and introduced her as well. Then he got to the point. 'You have a light for me to hang?'

'Yes.' She held the door open for them to pass through. 'But that's really enough payment for the puppy.'

His eyes went to Sammi's face. She was staring at him, her mouth opening and then closing, her teeth catching her lower lip.

He squeezed her hand before releasing it. '*That* was the surprise. Vonnie's dog had a litter of pups not too long ago, and she needed to find homes for them. I asked her to hold one in the hope that you'd accept it. For Toby.' He kept the money situation to himself.

'A puppy?' A smile started to form before it slid away. 'But, I can't…I couldn't.'

His fingers swept across her cheek, the skin smooth and silky to the touch. 'It'll be good for the boy to have a dog of his own. Please don't say no.'

She leaned into his hand. 'I won't. Thank you.'

Vonnie beamed. 'You can have your pick. They're chocolate Labs. I have two males and a female left in the litter.'

'Can I see them?' Sammi's voice held a hint of wonder, and Mark knew it was going to be all right. She was going to accept. If not for herself then for her child.

'Of course you can.' Aaron latched onto his mother's hand, popping his thumb into his mouth as he glanced from one to the other.

Vonnie led the way to the back of the house, through a closed door that passed through the kitchen. Behind a white child gate stood a beautiful Lab, her fur a glossy mahogany color that matched soft, liquid eyes. The animal gave a muted woof, her thick tail wagging back and forth. 'I have to keep them back here so Aaron doesn't bother them. He'd sleep with the little ones if he could.'

Reaching over the barrier, Vonnie stroked the dog's silky head. 'Her name is Brenda. She's wonderful with all people and with children especially. I imagine her pups will be the same.'

Sammi moved beside the woman and petted the animal. 'Hi, girl. Aren't you a beauty?'

The dog's tail made loud thumping sounds as it struck a

nearby wall with each and every wag, making the little boy squeal in delight. Vonnie laughed. 'That's her only downside. Her tail is a lethal weapon. She knocks over everything in reach. And if you get hit by it, it stings.'

Mark could well imagine. The animal's tail was thick and muscular, a classic sign of the breed, from what he'd read.

Vonnie unlatched the gate and, instead of barreling in and knocking the child over, Brenda came into the room and sat right in front of Aaron, her head lifting with a whine as if asking him to give her a pat. The child obliged and then wrapped his thin arms around her neck. The dog sighed and almost seemed to smile. Mark's chest tightened.

'The puppies are just inside. The males are normal sized, but the female is a runt. She's healthy but pretty small. She also has one ear that cocks up higher than the other.'

As soon as Sammi knelt in the midst of three brown squirming bodies, Mark knew which puppy she was going to choose. The female was in her arms in an instant, lapping at Sammi's face with little yips of excitement, her whole back end moving in time with her tail.

Vonnie peered round the corner and smiled. 'She's not worth as much as the other two as she's never going to be up to show standards, but she's as cute as a button.'

'She's perfect for Toby.' Sammi snuggled the pup closer.

Mark had to blink back the rush of emotion that came with the words. Sammi's awed voice said it all. Her son, who railed at his asthma, could learn so much from a dog that was considered less than perfect in some eyes.

But what about a man who was less than perfect? A man who had scars and nightmares and who still cringed at sudden sounds? Who had trouble looking at children like Aaron and Toby without remembering another child who would never grow up?

But while the puppy might be every bit as valuable as her two more robust siblings in Sammi's eyes and would become a wonderful companion, Mark wouldn't. He was missing some important pieces. He doubted he'd be a suitable companion for anyone.

Watching the two of them together, though, it was hard to make himself accept that fact.

'Is she old enough to leave her mother?'

Vonnie nodded. 'She's eight weeks old and weaned. I've already found homes for three of her littermates.'

He needed to get working on that light, before Sammi noticed his face. 'Where's that fixture you wanted hung?'

'Oh, it's in the living room. I've set a toolbox in there as well.' She glanced from one to the other. 'Would you like some coffee first?'

'Maybe in a little while.' He nodded toward Sammi. 'I think you're going to have to prise her out of there.'

Vonnie rubbed her tummy. 'I'm hoping to find them all homes before the baby comes.'

That's right. She was going to be all alone with a young child and a new baby. 'Your parents?'

'They're in Anchorage.' She bowed her head. 'I'll be moving back there once... I should have left earlier, but I just couldn't bring myself to say goodbye to this place. Greg and I worked hard on this home.'

'I'm sorry, Vonnie.'

She gave him a watery smile. 'I knew what I was getting into when I married him. We had three good years together before he was called to active duty.'

Unlike he and Sammi, who'd never gotten a real shot at happiness.

With one last glance at Sammi and the puppies, he pulled in deep breath. 'Why don't you show me the light fixture.'

Seated at the dinette table with a cup of coffee in front of her, Sammi smiled at the puppy curled up in her lap. The second she'd tried to put the young dog back in its bed with the others, the tiny animal had lifted her head and howled, glancing at Sammi out of the corner of her eye. She'd laughed and picked her up again, carrying the puppy with her into the kitchen. 'Don't think you're going to get this kind of treatment once you get home.'

The dog's ears perked as if to say, We'll see about that.

Mark was in the other room, balanced on top of a ladder, installing a new pendant light Vonnie's parents had sent for the house. 'Your light is going to be really pretty.'

'Much better than the bare bulb I've had hanging there for the last year.' Instead of coffee, the other woman nursed a glass of milk.

Sammi tried not to stare at her midsection, but it was impossible. Was that what she was going to look like eight months down the road?

No, because she was not pregnant. She'd even been snippy this morning with Mark. That had to prove she was heading for that time of the month. She'd never been really crabby or PMS-y, but right now she was willing to grab at any straw she could find.

Her hand headed for her tummy, something she'd found herself doing several times today, but she stopped it.

This is ridiculous. You're not pregnant!

Every time she repeated that mantra, something inside her shifted. Mourned for something that could never be.

Damn. What was wrong with her? If it had been with anyone else, she would have been horrified at the possibility.

And she was. But this was Mark. Someone she'd known since her childhood days. Someone she'd grown up with, laughed with…loved. Someone she…

Her throat grew tight as a sudden suffocating realization swept through her.

No. It can't be.

But it was.

She was in love with Mark. A man who'd left without a

backward glance eight years ago and had gone the speed-dating route in the six months he'd been back.

Only she hadn't heard rumors of him going out with *anyone* in the last month or two. And he'd blown off the nurse at the hospital. Why was that?

She listened to him work in the other room and tried to produce an ounce or two of self-righteous anger, but she couldn't. Because this was a man who cared enough about a pregnant widow to hang a light fixture for her. Who'd bought an IV warmer just because she had mentioned doing without. Who'd not only thought of Toby when he'd heard about this litter of puppies but had schemed with her mother and her colleagues to bring her on this outing. He'd brought warm donuts to her hotel room without being asked—had expressed outrage when he thought someone might have harmed her. And when he found out that no one had, had held her and…

Loved her.

She took a big gulp of her coffee, the liquid now cool, but she needed something to wash down the expanding lump that seemed stuck in her gullet.

And what was she going to do if she was indeed pregnant? Mark couldn't commit to a snowdrop if he were a snowman, so how in the world did she expect him to stick around to raise a child? And would she even want him to hang around for a reason like that?

No. If it came down to it, she'd raise this child on her own. She'd done it with Toby, she could do it again. And Vonnie was living proof that women were strong enough to handle just about anything.

Just then a rattling noise came from the living room, followed by a shout and then the sound of glass shattering. The adult dog rushed to the other room, while the pup in Sammi's lap lifted her head and whined softly.

After a split second of shock Sammi leaped up, holding the puppy in her arms, while Vonnie prised herself from her chair.

'Mark!'

A groan came from the other room.

Cradling the puppy, she hurried to the doorway, Vonnie right beside her.

Her free hand went to her throat just as Vonnie grabbed her dog's collar to prevent her from venturing further into the room. Sammi saw why in an instant.

The pendant light was up and lit, the glow from the light bulb making the linoleum floor glitter as if covered with thousands of tiny diamonds. Mark lay among them, gripping one of his arms.

Glass! Everywhere.

She spied the broken coffee table and overturned ladder. 'Oh, God, Mark, are you okay? What happened?'

'The boy! Where is he?' His glazed eyes latched onto hers. 'Have to stop the bleeding…too much blood.'

Sammi blinked, the panicked words making no sense. She then realized he was probably asking about Vonnie's son. 'Aaron's playing in his room, it's okay.'

It was as if she hadn't spoken. Mark gazed right through her, the expression on his face sending a chill through her. 'Ahmed! He's bleeding.'

It was then that something dripped off Mark's elbow and pinged silently against the floor, joining countless other drops that had already fallen. More were diving into the growing pool, the unmistakable scent of iron finally reaching her nose.

Blood. Lots of it.

CHAPTER SEVENTEEN

'I DON'T need stitches.' Mark's stubborn voice repeated the phrase.

Back at the plane, Sammi tamped down her rising exasperation. But it was better than the raw terror she'd felt when Mark had spouted off stuff that made no sense. He'd recovered within a couple of minutes, insisting he'd just been stunned from the fall.

She wasn't so sure. Yes, the names Ahmed and Aaron both started with the same letter, but there was no way in hell she'd confuse the two. She'd even checked Mark for a head injury, thinking he might have a concussion, but there was no sign of anything but the cut on his arm. Nothing that could explain what had happened in that living room.

'I think I know better than you do when a wound needs to be closed,' she snapped.

'You are not sewing me up. Just slap a butterfly on it, and I'll be good to go.'

'You're being ridiculous. It's in the crook of your elbow, Mark. If I don't suture it, you'll just keep opening it back up every time you bend your arm. The last thing you need is to have it get infected or not heal properly.' She reached for him. 'Besides, I want to look at it a little more closely.'

The puppy, safely tucked into an extra dog crate Vonnie had

on hand, whined. Sammi sighed. 'See? Even she knows you need stitches. Now, hop on the stretcher.'

Mark rolled his eyes, but did as she asked. He still seemed tense and distracted. 'It's only a little cut.'

Unwinding the bandages, which turned more and more crimson with every layer she removed, she glared at him. 'A little cut? I've seen some pretty nasty injuries caused by falls through glass tables.'

'I forgot the coffee table was behind the ladder. When I stepped off it, I caught the edge, and...' He shrugged. 'It broke.'

She bent over his arm. 'So did you. You're lucky you didn't slice through something important. Do you know how many nerves and vessels are located in this area?'

'No, but I'm sure you're about to enlighten me.'

His glare was acid, but in reality Sammi was relieved. The old Mark had returned with a vengeance.

She studied the wound. He'd cut all the way through his skin, revealing the rich red muscle tissue below but, despite the continued bleeding, nothing was spurting. 'Bend your fingers.'

Mark made a fist. 'Don't you think you're overreacting just a little?'

About this, or about that flight of fancy you went on a little while ago?

'No. And if I even suspect ligament or nerve damage, we're heading straight to Anchorage.'

'I have tourists to take back to Dutch Harbor, in case you've forgotten. In fact, they're due back in a couple of hours.'

'Then let me do my job, so you can do yours.' She didn't argue with him, but if this was serious, she wasn't going to wait around. They could radio the tourists and tell them to hightail it back in. Although asking Mark to fly a plane with a bad injury was suicidal. If she thought he was critical, she'd call for help. Blake could be here in four hours, if need be.

Laying a clean piece of gauze over the wound, she kept pressure on it as she assessed his tactile senses, making sure the nerves were still intact. She pressed one of his fingers with her free hand. 'Can you feel that?'

His white face and pinched lips turned in her direction. 'If you mean can I feel the cloth you're grinding into my cut, then damn straight. I feel it.'

'Sorry. I'll give you something for the pain in a minute.' She knew it hurt. But she hadn't wanted to inject him with lidocaine until she was sure she could do the stitching herself. She didn't want to cause any more damage than the glass had already done.

Keeping her voice calm, and her eyes on her work, she couldn't help but ask. 'Who's Ahmed?'

'Excuse me?'

'Ahmed. You called out his name when you were on the floor.'

He tried to pull his arm away, but she grabbed his wrist and held tight.

'I don't know what you're talking about.'

When she glanced into his face, she noted the bunched muscles in his jaw, the way his lips had thinned.

He was lying. He knew exactly who she was talking about, and it wasn't Vonnie's little boy.

'Mark?'

'Leave it alone.'

She sighed. He wasn't going to tell her anything. It was there in the stubborn set to his chin, the tight words.

'Fine, then take off your shirt.'

He finally met her gaze. 'I'm sorry?'

'Your sleeves are long and it's hard to maneuver around them.' She wasn't going to pry. From here on out, she'd show him nothing but professional interest.

'Right.' He helped her peel off the black sweater, the blood soaking his right sleeve not noticeable. Good thing. The tourist couple might be freaked out if they could see what Mark had done to himself.

She clenched her teeth, trying to remember her resolve as taut skin and toned muscle came into view, but the heat level in her tummy rose about ten degrees. Easing the piece of gauze away, she studied the injury itself. It was still oozing, but it was no longer dripping like it had been at Vonnie's when he'd talked about stopping the bleeding. About two inches long, the gash ran part way along the crease of his elbow and wrapped around to the outside. A piece of glass must have followed the curve of his arm as he'd gone down, because it hadn't sliced straight through to deeper tissues. He didn't know how lucky he was.

'I think it'll take seven or eight stitches. You okay with me doing them?'

'Come on, Sam. Are you sure this is necessary?'

'Yes. Are *you* going to make this as difficult as possible?'

One side of his mouth curved up, some of the tautness easing from his jaw. 'It's what I seem to be good at.'

'No kidding.' She grumbled the words while digging around for the supplies she needed, but underneath the growl a bit of her panic finally subsided. He could keep his secrets as long as he really was okay.

Sammi found everything then laid them beside Mark. 'I need to sterilize the area before I give the injection so I don't push any bacteria into your system. It's going to sting a bit.' Tipping the bottle, she sluiced alcohol over the wound, hearing his muffled curse as the liquid washed across his skin.

'You just want me to suffer as much as possible.'

For being so mean to her a little while ago? Yeah…maybe. 'What, a big bad navy pilot can't take a little sting?'

'Oh, I can take the little ones. It's the big ones that get to me.' Something dark peeked around the corners of his eyes, then sank back into the depths.

Her laughter died in her throat, and she drew some lidocaine into a syringe. 'You might want to look away. It makes it easier.'

'It really doesn't.' Again, there was something in the words that made her uneasiness come back in full force.

Was he talking about his father, and what the man had done to him? His time in the service?

Ahmed. The name whispered through her mind like puff of air then faded away.

Blake had never mentioned anything happening to Mark but, then she wasn't really sure they discussed those kinds of things, even within their own ranks. Shaking off the feeling, she slid the needle into the cut and pushed the plunger, working it slowly back out as she did. She repeated the stick a couple more times, never once feeling him wince as she did, even though he'd complained about the alcohol not three minutes earlier.

Maybe she should put in a call to Blake and see if the name Ahmed rang a bell, or if he knew anything.

She immediately dismissed it. Would Mark really appreciate her digging into something he was so reluctant to talk about?

Hardly.

Once she was satisfied he wouldn't feel anything, she threaded the suture material through the tiny needle and started closing the injury, taking her time and making sure she lined each flap of skin up as best she could. 'You're going to have a little scar, sorry.'

'Plenty more where that came from.' This time it wasn't her imagination. She'd definitely heard a hint of bitterness in his voice as he'd said it. You'd think he had tons of the things. But she'd studied every inch of that gleaming bronzed skin as they'd made love and aside from a single sickle-shaped scar marring the hard flesh of his left pec, he was about as good as they came. So if it wasn't a physical scar, what was it? Emotional?

Mark didn't seem like the type of man to dwell on what had happened to him as a child. Yes, his father had been a piece of work, but Mark had been able to function in school. And he'd never had an episode like the one in Vonnie's living room.

Her eyes widened. Neither had he ever gotten that haunted

look he'd had when Hannah had been injured. He'd frozen up then as well.

Damn. So many questions. But she didn't dare ask.

She finished stitching him up as quickly as she could and tied the last knot, checking her work. Not bad. It should heal cleanly. 'You'll want to come into the clinic in a week to have those taken back out.'

'I'll just take them out myself.'

She moved around in front of him until he met her eyes. 'Don't. You. Dare.'

He laughed, and the sound made her nerves again settle into place. 'Okay, Doc. Point taken.'

'Good.'

Setting her instruments into a metal tray then dropping the whole thing into a plastic bag to be sterilized later, she wet a clean piece of gauze and gently scrubbed the caked blood from his elbow, sliding the cloth down his forearm as she followed the trail. She did the same with his hand, dipping in and around each finger, leaning close to check for more places the stuff had dripped. 'Almost done.'

'Sam.'

The low murmured sound of her name caused her to glance up at him. 'What?'

There was no hint of the man who'd sent her into a panic an hour earlier. Instead, the Mark from the hotel room was back, eyes burning. 'I think you've done enough.'

It was then she realized his pupils had widened, almost obliterating the green of his irises. Before she fully absorbed his meaning, his uninjured hand came up and cupped the back of her head, fingers easing through her hair.

Her voice came out as a squeak when his meaning hit her. 'My patients don't normally react this way to getting stitches.'

'No?' The one syllable held a wealth of meaning. 'How do they react?'

'Mostly by groaning. Moaning. Sometimes cursing.'

He chuckled again. 'You're not helping me here, Sam. I can imagine myself doing each and every one of those things. For very different reasons.'

With that, he tugged her head down until her lips were a breath away from his. 'But for now I have a better idea. Let's see exactly which of those I can make *you* do.'

Mark heard the ooing and ahhing from the back of the plane as the tourists played with Sammi's new puppy. But his attention wasn't on what was happening in the back but what was going on in the seat beside his.

Sammi couldn't seem to get comfortable, shifting from side to side, looking anywhere but at him.

It made him feel like a first-class bastard. He wouldn't tell her about Ahmed when she'd asked, but he'd had no qualms about kissing her…and more. What was worse was that he'd pulled her towards him partially to stop her from probing further, but things had spiraled out of control. Just like they had in Vonnie's living room.

The second he'd seen the blood on the floor, the horrific scene from the back of his chopper had come to mind. He couldn't even remember what he'd said, but he must have said the boy's name…scared Sam enough to make the name stick.

Why couldn't he tell her?

Because it would be tantamount to voicing aloud what he'd never admitted even to himself: that he was having trouble dealing with what had happened on his plane that day. Yes, his dreams had eased, and he hadn't had one about Sam in almost a week. But it was as if his mind was playing a cruel joke, pulling back on a stretched rubber band and then letting it snap when he least expected it.

If he even suspected his flying would be affected or that he was putting people in danger, he'd stop going up. But the air was the one place where his concentration was so fixed on the tasks needing completion that it left no room for anything else.

What was he doing?

He'd made love to her. On his plane. And while it didn't quite qualify for the mile-high club, he was pretty sure he'd floated higher than that afterwards.

And it made him edgy. Because he had no idea what Sammi was thinking. Almost as soon as she'd caught her breath, she'd been clearing away the remainder of the medical materials she'd used while stitching his elbow, leaving him seated on the stretcher unable to move a muscle.

'Hey,' he said through the headset, knowing that while she could hear him, his passengers couldn't. 'Are you okay?'

Shift. Shift. Shift.

It took a full minute for her to actually turn and look at him. 'Fine.' Her face colored, glancing at the seats a few yards behind theirs. 'You don't think they know, do you?'

His gaze fell to the collar of her shirt and the mark hidden just beneath the fabric, remembering the way she'd squirmed, a moan coming from the far reaches of her stomach as he'd bitten down on the sensitive flesh.

Tell her!

He wanted to…wanted her to understand why he couldn't…

Hell, he loved the woman, knew the emotions had never truly disappeared even after all the time apart. And he could do nothing about it.

He settled for answering her question. 'No, they don't know.'

Her eyes clouded, her hands going to her braid and tugging it to the side. 'Let's get something straight. We've been down this road once before, and it didn't have a good ending. I'm not looking to repeat the mistakes I made in the past.'

Mistakes she'd made. Did she really consider their time together a mistake?

Who was he to ask something like that? Hadn't he treated it like one by taking off eight years ago? By never once writing her or telling her the truth after his father had died and he'd come back to Dutch Harbor?

Wasn't he treating today as a mistake by keeping his past a secret?

He could tell her the truth about why he'd left all those years ago. The truth about what happened on his chopper.

Where did he start?

Maybe it was better to start in the near past and work his way back to the distant past—if he even got that far.

He put his hands on the yoke of the plane and squeezed, trying to drum up the courage to do now what he should have done eight years ago.

Before he could back out, he opened his mouth, letting the words come out in a rush.

'Ahmed was a boy I knew in Afghanistan. His father was one of our medical translators, until insurgents found out he was helping us and gunned him down in front of his house. In front of his family. We felt responsible—if he hadn't been seen with us...' He swallowed before continuing. 'His wife was left with nothing but their son. We got together and took up a collection, buying food and helping to pay Ahmed's tuition in a private elementary school. We moved them to another part of the city. A place we thought they'd be safe.'

But they hadn't been. The insurgents had tracked them down hell bent on making her pay for accepting the 'infidels'' help, as they called all the UN troops. They'd wounded Ahmed and strapped his mother with a bomb, knowing she'd run right to his squadron to get help for her boy. She'd been smarter than they had, though, setting her son on the ground about a hundred yards away from Mark's chopper. She'd run the other way just as the bomb had gone off...

Why tell Sammi any more than he already had, though? He'd admitted to knowing the boy and helping him. She could make believe the story had a happy ending. Just the way he sometimes imagined it.

Only he evidently wasn't all that convincing, even to himself, as evidenced by his nightmares. Or by the way he'd called out Ahmed's name the second he'd fallen through that coffee table. He'd heard the explosion of glass and had thought it was the damned bomb all over again.

Sammi was staring at him, her brow puckered as she waited for him to continue, trying to put the pieces together all by herself. Suddenly a look of horror slid through her eyes, her hand coming up to cover her mouth for a long moment.

Then she reached out, her fingers going to his on the yoke and prising them loose, holding them tight in her own.

'Ahmed died, didn't he?'

CHAPTER EIGHTEEN

SAMMI waited in the hangar as Mark took care of the plane and his passengers, her mind a jumble of shock and dismay. The puppy was fast asleep in the animal crate by her feet, his soft breathing rising to meet her ears.

That poor child.

The second she'd asked the question, she'd known it was the truth. The boy had died. Mark hadn't denied it, neither had he responded, but his hand had given hers a quick squeeze before releasing her to scrub the back of it over his eyes.

The man had been on the verge of tears.

It was unthinkable. The happy-go-lucky, fun-loving guy who'd come home from the navy, duffle bag slung over one shoulder and a big smile plastered to his face as he'd disembarked, wasn't as carefree as he seemed. Had it all been an act—his way of dealing with the horrors he'd lived through overseas?

Had he talked to anyone about all this?

Before she could process her thoughts and organize them, Mark joined her, reaching behind her to tweak her braid. 'Ready to go?'

No, she didn't want to go anywhere until they could sit down and have a heart-to-heart discussion, but Toby was due home from school in about a half hour. Besides, there was something in her that needed to hug her son tightly and give him a silent promise that no one would ever hurt him. Even the thought brought an ache to her chest that squeezed harder and harder until she couldn't breathe. So she said the only thing she could right now: 'Yes, I'm ready.'

His eyes searched hers for a second, and she willed herself not to break down and sob in front of him. Somehow she knew that was the worst thing she could do. He'd take it as a sign that she pitied him for what he'd had to endure.

She didn't pity him. She hurt for him in a way she'd never hurt for another human being in her life. Not her ex-husband, not her patients...not even her son. She ached for the man who'd done his damnedest to help a family and had ended up feeling like he'd hurt them instead.

Mark was silent as he drove Sammi back to the clinic. She struggled to find something to say, but everything she came up with just seemed shallow and trite. She wanted to ask him to pull over and let her hold him, but she didn't.

How did you heal a wound that had become part of the man himself?

Maybe you didn't. Maybe you simply acknowledged the scar without trying to pick it back open again.

They pulled into the parking lot, and Sammi put her hand through the crook of his uninjured arm and leaned her head against his shoulder. He stiffened for the tiniest fraction of a second before relaxing. 'What's this for?'

She sat back up. 'I just felt like it.'

'Thanks.'

'You're welcome.' She paused, trying to figure out where they went from here, or if they even did. There was a fork in the road, and Sammi wasn't sure which path to choose.

Could she risk her heart and Toby's on a man who might never be quite whole?

She wasn't sure. She'd slept with the man twice, might even be carrying his child. A decision had to be made.

And if he decided he didn't want a relationship?

One way or the other, she had to tell him the truth. Which meant, if she hadn't started her period within a week or so, she'd have to choose a venue. Since she didn't know when she would see him again, it was better to go ahead and plan something.

Could she do it?

'Listen,' she said, trying to find her way in unfamiliar territory, 'you wouldn't be interested in having a picnic with me and Toby, would you?'

She held her breath as she waited on his response.

'You want to go on a picnic this time of year?'

That didn't sound very promising. 'I never said it had to be outside. We could have it at my place. Just throw a couple of blankets on the floor and have some traditional grub. Fried chicken. Potato salad. I'll do all the cooking.'

He shifted to look at her. 'How could I refuse an offer like that?'

Her breath left her lungs in a relieved whoosh. 'I do make a pretty mean fried chicken.'

'When were you thinking?'

'Shall we plan it for Friday afternoon? Toby won't have school the next day.'

Hmm…that could be taken the wrong way. Maybe she should clarify things. 'I wouldn't feel comfortable having you spend the night with my son in the next room, though. Not at his age.' She smiled to soften the words, but tensed when he didn't smile back.

'Of course not.'

She gave a nervous laugh and tried to backtrack a little bit further, in case she'd insulted him. 'Okay, so you might have to remind me about the no-spending-the-night clause. Because I have a feeling you may be stronger in that area than I am.'

The first hint of a smile pulled at the corners of his lips. 'I doubt that, Sam. I sincerely doubt that.'

* * *

Sammi stared at the pregnancy test in her hands.

The week at the clinic had flown by, despite the fact that Mark hadn't put in an appearance. It was just as well. She needed time and a little bit of space to think things through. Was she wrong to put herself in a situation like this? The man had hurt her once. And she was more than a little vulnerable at the moment as she was now over a week late with her period.

Why now? Why not next year, when she was better able to tell what Mark was thinking—see how he acted?

Still staring at the test, she tried to get up the courage to actually take it. If she was pregnant, it was early on, but this particular test was pretty sensitive to any shift in hormones. Did she really want to do this now? Wouldn't it be better to wait a while longer so she could have plausible deniability in case things went horribly wrong on their picnic?

Yes. But she wasn't sure it was the right thing to do.

Just take it and get it over with. It's killing you not to know.

Firming her resolve, she went into the small restroom at the clinic and locked the door. Putting her hands on the edge of the sink, she leaned forward and stared at herself in the mirror.

You might be having Mark's baby. How do you feel about that?

Elated. Terrified.

She smiled at her reflection. But most of all full of hope.

The test strip came out of the package and she eyed the blank space where she would soon see a pink plus or a blue minus.

No time like the present. She went into the stall and sat on the toilet for a few seconds before getting up the nerve to actually do the deed. Once she did, the second temptation was to toss it into the medical waste receptacle without giving it a glance. But she didn't.

She left the stall and laid the strip on top of the box, washing her hands and then splashing cool water over her face. Her reflection no longer smiled back at her, but was pale and sober. Somehow she already knew without having to look.

Still, she took a deep breath and blew it back out, then forced her eyes to the little plastic case.

The first thing that stood out was the color. Pink. She didn't need to see the plus to know what it meant.

She was pregnant. *They* were pregnant.

And Sammi had no idea how to break the news to Mark.

Something was wrong.

Mark wasn't sure how he knew, but there was a hitch in Sammi's smile as she sat on the blanket across from him—and that smile seemed overly bright, even to his untrained eyes. And beneath her quick laugh lay a serious undertone that made him wonder if she'd changed her mind.

Maybe she was regretting asking him here.

Who could blame her? He'd hurt her once before, maybe she wasn't going to give him the chance to do it again. But he'd done a lot of thinking. He hadn't had a nightmare all week. Maybe Sammi was good for him. Maybe this was what he needed.

The problem was, how could he prove to her that he wasn't out to repeat the mistakes of the past?

And leaving her had been a mistake. No matter what his father had said or done, he should have been honest with her. But he hadn't wanted what they'd had to be tainted by threats or be afraid for Sammi's safety every time he was out of the house.

Maybe they could have even run away together. But he'd been too terrified to think straight at the time. He'd just wanted to get as far away as possible, giving his dad no reason to set his sights on Sammi. He'd wanted to keep her safe.

The way he and his buddies had tried to keep Ahmed and his mother safe?

He realized now that something terrible could have happened to Sammi while he'd been away. But it hadn't. His father hadn't dared touch anyone outside his immediate family, because then someone might finally discover his secret.

Shaking off his thoughts, he scraped the last of the potato salad from his plate and popped it into his mouth. 'Delicious. Is there more of this stuff?'

Toby eyed him, his small nose wrinkling. 'It has mayonnaise in it, you know.'

'Yes, it does.' Mark kept his voice serious, trying not to let the smile that tumbled around in his gut come to the surface. His feelings for the boy had grown over the past month, the real child overshadowing any likeness to Ahmed. 'I happen to like mayonnaise.'

'Yuck. It tastes like white slime.'

'Toby.' Sammi's voice held a light warning as she scooped more potato salad onto Mark's plate. 'Remember what we talked about? Not everyone has the same likes and dislikes as you.'

'I know.' He picked up his chicken leg and took a big bite out of it, glancing at his puppy, who'd been corralled in a playpen.

Belly—Sammi said the name Bella had morphed into Belly, due to the puppy's round stomach and the fact that she was always hungry—seemed to sense her master's attention and took the opportunity to whine.

Funny that Sammi had kept the playpen around long after Toby had outgrown it. She'd also kept that baby wipe warmer she'd mentioned a while back. Something about the smiling moons on a dark blue background made him nervous. Would Sammi want more children someday? He had been so sure he'd never want any of his own after his time in the Middle East. And yet here he was with Toby, smiling and almost completely at ease.

Almost.

He turned his attention to Sammi, reaching out to touch her hand. 'Everything okay?'

'Fine.' Bright smile. The same one she'd flashed the last two times he'd asked that question.

'Are you regretting having me over?' Despite the baby contraption across the room, sitting on the ancient quilt in the middle of Sammi's living room felt right. Too right.

'No. Oh, no.' She wrapped her fingers around his, squeezing tight. 'I know I seem distracted. It's just a lot to absorb, you know? Two months ago we were standing at Molly and Blake's wedding doing everything we could not to even look at each other, and now we might be having...' Her eyes widened, her voice falling away.

'We might be having what?'

Toby's head came up, his jaws grinding yet another bite of chicken. 'Yeah, we might be having what?'

Sammi sighed and pulled her hand away to ruffle her son's hair. 'You, my dear, have very big ears.'

'I do not!' He reached up to finger one of his ears, a line of worry puckering the skin between his brows. 'Do I?'

She leaned down to kiss his head. 'No, silly. That's another way to say that you hear everything that goes on around you.'

'My teacher says I'm a great listener.'

'She does indeed.' Sammi glanced at Mark and gave him the knowing smile that one parent might give to another. He allowed himself to relax.

Belly yipped, then gave a mournful howl.

'Mom, can we let her out yet?'

'When everyone's done eating. Plates on the floor are too much of a temptation for that little lady.'

Mark scraped the last of his potato salad onto his fork and slid it into his mouth, then swallowed. 'Better than any restaurant could have made.'

'There's nothing quite like home-made.'

He reached out and touched her face, loving the smoothness of her skin. 'You're right. There's also nothing quite like home.'

'No. There really isn't.' She studied him. 'Does this feel like home? Being back on the island, I mean.'

'It didn't when I first came back.' He couldn't resist leaning forward to drop a quick kiss on her cheek. 'But it does now.'

'I'm glad.' She reached over to gently close Toby's gaping mouth, bringing a smile to Mark's face. 'Now, I think we should get this cleaned up so Belly Bella can come out to play.'

Helping Sammi pick up the plates and serving bowls, the feeling of rightness still hung in the air. That had to be a good thing, didn't it? He hadn't felt the urge to slam through the front door and flee into the night yet. Neither had he pictured flaming helicopters filled with wounded soldiers at every turn. He'd even been a little less jumpy over the past week.

Every day seemed to have wrought more and more of a change in his heart and mind. Puttering around his house seemed unbearably lonely, even though he still made it a point to check in on his mother every day. He was encouraged by the fact that she seemed to be getting out of the house more and mingling with her old friends.

What would she think about all this?

She'd definitely approve. She'd wanted Mark to settle down for a long, long time. There was no way she could understand why he hadn't, or why his legs had turned rubbery when he'd pulled that ring box out of the back of his sock drawer.

Was he actually thinking of…?

Yes. He'd clicked open the top of that box more than once over the last week. But it was too soon. He needed to take things slower than they had the first time. But despite wrenching open his closet door and letting her see the big bad skeleton he'd hidden inside, she hadn't looked at him any differently. Hadn't kept Toby close to her side as if afraid he might snap under the pressure at any second.

His heart swelled with love that what he'd once thought impossible might be not only possible but easier than he'd ever imagined. Sammi had invited him to her house to eat with her and Toby. That had to mean she cared at least a little, right?

They got everything up off the floor just in time for Toby to reach into the playpen and lift out the tiny dog. Racing around the room a time or two, she skidded on the tile floor, paddling with her legs until she finally got them back under herself.

Mark bent down and scrubbed behind the pup's ears, then lifted one of her paws, staring at the oversized pads. 'Have you seen the size of these? She might have been the runt, but I have a feeling she's going to catch up, and fast. She's already grown since the last time I saw her.'

'They don't stay small for ever,' Sammi murmured, putting her hand on Toby's head.

The doorbell rang, startling him. Belly took off for the entrance, four legs going in all directions, looking like a cross between a drunken ice-skater and cross-country skier.

Standing, he glanced at Sammi, who gave him a quick smile. 'Toby, get your backpack, honey, Grandma's here.'

'Why would he need to—?'

'My mom's agreed to watch Toby and Belly for the night.'

His brain tried to compute as Sammi started for the front door. Just before she opened it, she looked back at him. 'Like I said at the clinic, I never claimed to be the strong one.'

CHAPTER NINETEEN

SAMMI sat up quickly, the sheets tangled around her. The room was dark, and she tried to figure out what had awoken her. A rustling to her left met her ears, followed by a groan.

Mark.

She started to turn toward him, but his legs—hidden somewhere beneath the covers—jerked, freezing her in place. A pained growl issued from his chest, sending a chill skittering down her spine. Not quite a wail, the sound was low and feral—like an animal that had been cornered and was fighting for its life.

He must be dreaming. She blinked the rest of the way awake, letting her eyes adjust to the darkness.

Naked. Why was she...?

It all came rushing back. The night before, her mom had taken Toby and Belly home with her, giving Sammi a knowing wink when she saw Mark standing behind her. Then, finally alone with him, she'd led him back to her bedroom, where they'd spent hours rediscovering all those secret places they had once known. No stolen moments, no rushing. Just her... and Mark.

He'd tried to leave afterwards, murmuring that he didn't want Toby to find them in the morning.

No need, she'd said. Toby wouldn't be back until tomorrow afternoon. He'd tensed, but in the end had allowed himself to be coaxed back to bed. Besides, she couldn't let him leave without telling him about the baby. She'd meant to do it beforehand, but he'd looked at her with such need that she'd decided to follow his lead.

His thrashing grew more intense, and she placed her hand on his chest to wake him up. 'Mark?'

His reaction wasn't what she expected. He lunged up from the mattress, grabbed her arms and rolled over on top her, his naked body pressing hers deep into the soft surface. She gave a little screech at the suddenness of the move but arched toward him to show him she was more than willing. Instead of feeling that ready heat pressing against her center, she was shocked to find him soft. No sign of the urgency that vibrated off the rest of his body.

Well, she could fix that. She tried to move her hand down his stomach, but found she couldn't.

What was happening?

'Mark?' She looked into his face, realizing his fingers weren't just snug around her upper arms, they were actually tightening more as the seconds passed, hurting her. His mouth moved, but no sound came out.

She tried to gain some wiggle room and failed. 'Are you okay?'

No response. It was as if he hadn't heard her.

Panic welled up inside of her, along with a sense of claustrophobia she hadn't felt since she'd allowed friends to bury her in the sand as a young child. They'd run off, leaving her trapped and helpless. This was the exact same sensation.

'Mark, let me up, you're scaring me.'

'You won't get her.' The words were a low snarl.

Terror clogged her pores, collected in her lungs, and she began struggling in earnest, bucking beneath him and finally letting out a scream that could have woken the dead.

And it did. Mark stiffened above her, then rolled away, the pressure on her chest gone, leaving her gasping down huge lungfuls of air. Her heart gave a series of palpitations as the surge of adrenaline eased.

She sat up, her hand at her throat as she turned to look at him.

He hadn't bothered to cover himself, and lay on the bed completely exposed, his arm thrown over his eyes. Deep shudders wracked his body, which was slick with sweat.

Fear morphed into concern. 'Mark?'

'Don't say anything.' His voice shook, but at least it was his own again. Not that mindless creature who'd hulked over her looking like he wanted nothing more than to strangle the life out of her.

She touched him, and he flinched, then he moved his arm and let her see into his eyes, which were deep pools of anguish.

'Wh-what happened?' she asked.

'I had a dream.'

Holy hell.

'*That* was a dream?'

'I have them sometimes. It's why I didn't want to stay over.' He turned his head to look at her. 'I'm sorry for scaring you.'

He'd done more than frighten her. And his words told her those so-called 'dreams' happened often enough that he was wary about spending the night anywhere. Was that why he'd dated so many women? Because he knew what could happen if he got too involved? If they wanted him for longer than just an hour or two? 'Why didn't you say something last night?'

'Because I hadn't had one in a while. I thought it was safe.'

What if Toby had been in the house? What if he'd heard her scream and had come running into the room to find Mark leaning over her like a maniac?

She swallowed. Or what if Toby had come into the room and saw Mark moving in his sleep and tried to wake him up? Would Mark have lashed out at her son without realizing what he was doing? What if she'd been further along in her pregnancy and he'd somehow hurt the baby?

She'd told him she'd never let anyone hurt her or her child. Did she mean what she said? Even if that 'anyone' was Mark Branson himself? Someone she loved? Someone she was pretty sure might feel something toward her as well?

Her thoughts rolled over and over, tangled and chaotic.

'Have you talked to anyone about these dreams?'

He sat up and scrubbed a hand through his hair. 'I don't need to. They're just dreams.'

Were they? She thought about his other odd behavior. Like calling out Ahmed's name at Vonnie's house and the way he'd zoned out during Hannah's injury. They had to be connected.

Flashbacks, maybe?

'You can't be serious, Mark.' She laid her hand back on his chest, his heartbeat pounding against her palm. 'Are these dreams about your time in the military? About Ahmed?'

'You wouldn't understand.'

She pushed forward, not allowing him to brush off her concerns. 'You're right. There's probably no way I could. But someone will. There are people who are trained to—'

'No.' Swinging his feet off the bed, he found his briefs and tugged them up over his lean hips. His other clothing followed in short order, leaving her with the sheet pulled up to her waist.

'Mark, let's talk about this.' Sammi had so much she wanted to know, desperately wanted to understand what was going on in his head.

'Nothing to talk about. This was a mistake.' He picked his wallet up off the nightstand and stuffed it into the back pocket of his jeans.

A mistake. She recoiled against the headboard, her hand automatically going to her stomach as if to protect the child inside. Then she pulled the sheet up to cover her breasts, although the act did nothing to make her feel any less naked and exposed.

Would he consider their baby a mistake as well? Want nothing to do with it?

He moved toward the door in the dark and put his hand on the knob.

Turned it.

'I'm pregnant.'

She'd planned to do this gently, break the news to him after serving him breakfast in bed. But he was leaving, and unless she could do something to change his mind, he might never come back. Never know the truth.

Mark went very still then looked at her, his eyes glittering from across the room. 'What did you say?'

'I—I'm pregnant.' She gripped the sheets harder, wondering if the Egyptian cotton she'd splurged on a few years ago would withstand the strain. But nothing ripped.

Except her heart.

Because after the briefest of pauses, when she could have sworn he was going to respond to her words, he swore softly instead. Then he pushed through the door, leaving her more alone than she'd ever been in her life.

Sammi took her time showering, allowing the water to cascade over her. If only it could wash away her tears as easily as it did her shampoo. But nothing could erase them, because they weren't pouring from her tear ducts but were locked deep inside her, in a remote corner of her heart.

Her eyes remained dry as she dressed, taking the time to do her hair and make-up. They stayed dry on the trip to Mark's house, where she parked in front of his white garage door.

She sat there for several minutes, trying to drum up the courage to go and knock on the door. His car was there, so she knew he was home.

Sucking down a deep breath, she finally climbed out of her car. Before she made it halfway up the walk, the front door opened and Mark stood there, one hand on top of his door-frame, watching her approach.

Neither of them said a word as she reached him.

'I'm not here to ask you for anything. You had a right to know.'

'I appreciate you telling me.'

Those words told her nothing.

Sammi swallowed, not sure exactly how to do what she'd come to do. 'I care about you, Mark. More than I should, probably. But I want you to think back to that day in the hotel room when you asked about Brad. I told you I wouldn't let anyone hurt Toby or me. Do you remember?'

'Yes.'

'You scared me this morning.'

'I've already apologized for that.' His face was an empty mask, the words slow and mechanical.

'Yes. You did.' Her mind blanked out for a second or two as she faced her future, the front stoop doing a slow twirl as if circling an imaginary drain.

Stop it.

She forced herself to stand up straight and continue. She had to do this now or she'd back out. 'I can't risk Toby seeing what I saw—or worse. Not with his asthma.'

Mark didn't say anything, but the color drained from his face.

Sammi's heart squeezed inside her, agony turning her blood to dust in her veins. 'I don't know how you feel about us...about me. But I can't get involved with someone whose refusal to admit he might have a problem makes him a danger not only to himself but to those he's around.'

A muscle worked in his jaw. 'I'm sure you're getting around to saying something profound.'

Damn him! How could he stand there and act like none of this mattered? Like she didn't matter?

Because she didn't. It was why he'd been able to walk away from her eight years ago with barely a wave of his hand.

She backed up a step, anger flaring through her system. 'You always were a smart guy, Mark. You're right. I'm getting around to saying this: unless you talk to someone about what's going on with you, I don't want to see you again. I don't want to fly with you on medevacs. And I especially don't want you stopping by to see Toby. Understood?'

A few seconds of silence blanketed the area then his hand came off the doorframe, and he took a step forward, winding up on the front stoop, mere inches from where she stood. Something dark pooled behind his pupils, turning them inky black as he stared down at her.

Panic skittered up her spine, but she didn't move from her spot. She was not going to stumble back to her car like a frightened little mouse. He wasn't going to hurt her. He might be a soldier, but he was still a man, and she knew her words had struck deep.

He'd confided in her on their trip home from Umnak, and again this morning, and now she was using those confessions against him. Maybe he thought she was holding the pregnancy over his head as emotional blackmail. But the baby had nothing to do with this. Not really.

This was about Mark.

How much was she willing to bet on her position…on the belief that she was right?

As he went back inside without a word and shut the door behind him with a soft click, she had her answer about what she was giving up.

Everything.

CHAPTER TWENTY

BLAKE met him at the airport. 'Are you sure about this?'

'No, but I don't have a choice.' The blow Sammi had dealt had sent him into a spiral over the past couple of weeks.

What did she know? He was fine. Fine! She didn't want to see him again? Didn't want him near her kid? Well, that was fine, too. He'd chucked the ring to the farthest reaches of his closet and then cancelled all his flights for the foreseeable future.

He'd spent the majority of his time at the local watering hole, drinking away his cares. Or at least trying to. Then a drunk had slammed a glass down on the bar with a little too much enthusiasm, sending a loud crack of sound ricocheting to the corners of the bar. Mark had landed in a defensive crouch, fists raised, eyes darting from person to person. Only when he'd realized everyone was staring at him, that the place had gone deadly silent, did he realize what he'd done, and how far out of the norm it seemed to be for the world around him. His body may have come home from the war unscathed, but his mind seemed to have dragged something extra back with it. Something that had scared Sammi enough to order him to stay away from her.

Blake gripped his shoulder and looked into his face. 'Let's go, then. They're waiting for you.'

* * *

'Hannah! What's up, girl?'

Sammi held the cellphone against her ear as she stirred the hamburger helper, the one 'fun' food she permitted Toby to have every Friday night—doctored up, of course, with broccoli florets. Belly sat beside the stove, her doggy gaze fixed on the food preparations that were under way. Toby was in the living room, assembling the new construction set his father had given him on their last visit.

'I'm thinking of renting a movie,' her friend said. 'Are you game?'

'What movie?'

Four weeks and counting. Mark had evidently taken her at her word and was steering clear not only of her but the entire island. Rumor had it that he'd gone to Anchorage. Sammi had no idea if it was a permanent thing or if he was coming back. But she wasn't going to put her life on hold, waiting for something that might never materialize.

'What is Toby allowed to watch?'

'We try to stick to the three Gs around here.'

Hannah laughed. 'Do I even want to know what that means?'

'Yes, since it'll narrow your choices down to a manageable few.' She ticked off her fingers. 'Gore-less, Grunt-less, and Ghost-less.'

'Grunt-less?'

'You know…*grunting*.' She emphasized the word enough to let Hannah in on the codeword.

'Oh…grunting.' Hannah laughed. 'Well, that knocks out all the fun movies.'

'Sorry about that.' She crooked her shoulder to hold the phone as she dished some food onto Toby's plate and walked over to the tiny dinette table. She motioned to him, pointing at the food. He leaped up and came running…and so did Belly. 'Hold on a second, would you?'

She grabbed the dog just before she tried to scramble onto

the chair ahead of Toby. 'Where do you think you're going, young lady?'

Carrying the pup to the playpen, she set her inside, realizing just how fast the dog was growing. Soon she'd be big enough to leap out of the confined area. But it was just as well. She'd have to sterilize the playpen to use for the baby. She'd shared her secret with Hannah and Molly, but no one else. She couldn't. Not quite yet. She'd eventually have to tell her mother, which wasn't going to be a lot of fun.

Making sure Toby was eating, she put the phone back to her ear. 'Sorry about that. I had to—' The sound of the doorbell pealing stopped her in mid-sentence.

Good heavens. Why did things always come in waves?

'Hannah, I have to get the door. Can I call you back?'

'It's okay, I'll call you from the movie store.'

'You sure?'

'Yep. Talk to you soon.'

'Okay. Don't forget the rules—' she swung the door open '—I told you about…' She stared in disbelief, the phone falling from her hand and clattering to the floor.

'Sammi? Sammi?' She heard Hannah's voice calling out to her but couldn't tear her eyes from the person in front of her.

Mark, a little bit thinner than he'd been four weeks ago, stared at her. 'I'm back.'

'So I see,' she whispered. Why was he there?

He nodded at the floor, where Hannah's voice was growing more distressed. 'You'd better get that.'

Sammi swallowed, then bent down to retrieve the phone. 'Sorry, Hannah. I—I dropped the phone.'

'You scared me to death. Is everything all right?'

She searched Mark's eyes, seeing the corners crinkle as he gave her a slight smile. 'You know what? I think it just might be, but we'll have to cancel our movie plans for tonight, okay? I'll talk to you later.'

Clicking the phone shut and stepping through the entryway

so that Toby wouldn't see Mark before she had a chance to find out what was going on, she pulled the door closed behind her. She'd told him not to contact her again, unless…

Could it be?

She waited, but he didn't seem in any hurry to say anything, his eyes trailing over her as if he couldn't get enough.

'How's Toby? The baby?' he asked.

Hearing him acknowledge their child sent a flash of joy shooting through her system, which she immediately tried to tamp down. 'They're both fine.'

He nodded. 'I did as you asked. I went to see a therapist. In Anchorage. Someone who specializes in post-traumatic stress disorder. Blake went to the same guy after he got out of the navy.'

A feeling of shock went through her. Blake had gone to a therapist too?

'How did it go?'

'I learned that some things shouldn't be handled on your own. That lots of other guys have the same issues. It's not just about me being too weak to handle things on my own.'

'Weak?' She closed the gap between them and leaned her head on his chest. 'You're not weak. *God,* Mark. You're the strongest man I've ever known.'

His cheek came down to rest on top of her head. 'I love you, Sammi. I always have. Always will.'

'Always?' She leaned back to look at him, not sure she'd heard him right. 'But…but you left. Why?'

He let go of her and reached into his pocket and pulled out a little box. Cracking it open, she saw the ring inside, its small stone glittering up at her. 'Because my father found this in my room. Said some things that led me to believe that my being involved with you could put you in danger.'

'My God.' She stared at the ring, not believing he'd bought it all those years ago. Her heart went to her throat and stuck there. 'Why didn't you tell me?'

'Because I knew you'd try to talk me out of leaving. I realize now it wasn't the smartest move, but we were both young. I didn't know what else to do at the time.'

There was a tiny part of her that wondered if this was really happening. If Mark Branson was really standing on her doorstep, declaring his undying love for her. She blinked the world in and out of focus. Still there. 'You had this ring eight years ago? You kept it all this time?'

'Yes.'

She leaned back, pulling in a deep breath to let his scent fill her, surround her. All the hurt and bitterness of the past faded away. He was real. He loved her. 'Why are you showing it to me now?'

'Because I hoped that you might...' He ground to a halt. 'I don't want you to think I went to see someone just because you told me to. I did it for me. For us.'

'Is there an "us"?'

He nodded. 'I hope so.'

'So do I. I love you too, Mark. I don't think I ever stopped.'

He pulled her tight against him for a long moment. This time the sensation wasn't scary. It filled her with hope. Joy. So many other things.

'I know this is too soon but...' he let her go and prised the ring from its velvety bed '...would you consider becoming my wife? I still have a lot of work to do, and I'll want you there with me for some of my sessions, so you'll know what to expect—how to help me as I recover.'

Tears blurred her vision. 'I'll be right there beside you, every step of the way.'

'No more running. No more lies.' He folded her in his arms and kissed the top of her head.

She reached up on tiptoe and kissed him back, her lips searching his, clinging to them when he immediately deepened the kiss. By the time she pulled back, gasping for breath, she was laughing. 'I'd better remember those three Gs myself.'

When he looked at her, puzzled, she shook her head. 'I'll explain later. Come inside. I know Toby's going to want to see you.' Everything else could wait: explanations, discussions about the future.

'Wait a second.' He took her left hand and lowered himself to one knee. 'Samantha Grey Trenton, I don't deserve you, but would you do me the honor of becoming my wife?'

The ring slipped onto her finger like magic, the fit perfect.

'Are you sure this is what you want?'

'It's all I've ever wanted.'

She smiled and drew him to his feet, her heart kicking up its heels and sprinting towards the finish line. 'Then welcome home, Mark. We're glad you're back.'

EPILOGUE

'I FOUND some!'

Toby's voice came from the other side of the salmonberry patch, interrupting the kiss Mark had tried to sneak from Sammi. She looked up at him with a smile, her growing belly pressed tightly against his, causing all kinds of strange and wonderful sensations inside his skull and elsewhere.

He couldn't get enough of her, even now when she was mere weeks away from delivering their child.

A little girl. They'd chosen Melody for her name, after his maternal grandmother, something Sammi had insisted on.

He'd finished his treatments for post-traumatic stress syndrome a few months ago, and Sammi, true to her word, had been right there for many of the sessions, which they'd scheduled for days when Toby was visiting his father. The nightmares were gone. And both he and Sammi had learned coping mechanisms in case any problems arose in the future.

Toby's shout came again, 'Mom! I found some!'

Mark nuzzled her cheek, nipping her earlobe. 'I think he found something.'

'Mmm,' she murmured. 'So did you.'

'Did I?' He kept his voice low. 'You know the doctor says we have to be good from here on out, until after the baby's born.'

'What does he know?' That little kitten purr she had drove him crazy with need, just like it always did.

Mark took a deep breath then stepped back, gritting his teeth as he tried to pull himself together.

'Party pooper,' she said.

'Hey, don't blame me.'

Sammi cupped her stomach. 'You see there, Melody? You daddy is blaming you for having to keep his—'

'Don't say it.'

'What? I was going to say "for having to keep his plane in the hangar".'

'Very funny.' They both knew she wasn't talking about his actual plane, which was also grounded until after the baby was born. He wasn't going to take any chances on her going into labor while he was off on a charter flight.

Belly and Toby came running toward them, Toby's mouth smeared with a suspicious red substance. 'Toby, I promised those berries to a doctor in Anchorage.'

'Sorry, Mom. I'll go and find some more.' He turned and raced away again, Belly hard on his heels.

Mark eyed her. 'Exactly how many pints of jam do you owe people?'

'Um…' She twisted her hands. 'Maybe thirty.'

'Thirty? And how do you expect to can thirty jars of jelly before you give birth?'

'Well…' She drew out the word as she looked him up and down.

'Oh, no. I don't know anything about making stuff like that.'

'I could talk you through it.'

Mark laughed, a rush of love spiraling through his chest as he looked at the beautiful woman he'd married a month ago. 'I'm sure you could. And just what would I get for my trouble?'

She sidled up to him and ran a finger down his chest, before hooking it into his waistband and giving a suggestive little tug. 'You'd get something *very* special. Something reserved for only a select few.'

His mouth went dry. 'Which is?

She gave him a slow smile. 'Why...a pint of salmon-berry jam.'

* * * * *